A Simple Deduction

Kristi Holl

Annie's®
AnniesFiction.com

Books in the Amish Inn Mysteries series

Library of Congress-in-Publication Data
A Simple Deduction/ by Kristi Holl
p. cm.
I. Title
                         2017947137

AnniesFiction.com
(800) 282-6643
Amish Inn Mysteries™
Series Creator: Shari Lohner
Series Editor: Jane Haertel
Cover Illustrator: Kelley McMorris

10 11 12 13 14 | Printed in China | 9 8 7 6

Liz Eckardt glanced at the kitchen clock—was it ten o'clock already?—and used her arm to push her hair out of her eyes. How had she gotten so far behind? This weekend she was hosting the first-ever mystery weekend at her bed-and-breakfast, the Olde Mansion Inn, and there was still a lot to do before her guests arrived. Speeding up, she chopped meat and vegetables, then added them to the frying pan on the stove.

She heard a door open and close from the front of the house, and a minute later a familiar hearty voice said, "What's that I smell?"

"Come on in, Sadie," Liz called. "I've got Dutch squash biscuits in the oven."

"Yum." Radiating her usual earthy good cheer, Sadie Schwarzentruber sniffed appreciatively. Sadie, along with her business partner, Mary Ann Berne, rented space from Liz on the ground floor of the inn for their quilt and sewing shop, Sew Welcome. "How's your mystery weekend shaping up?"

"Barring unforeseen circumstances, I'll be ready when the guests arrive at three this afternoon." She stirred the frying meat and vegetables. "Your help writing the play script was invaluable."

"We had a blast," Sadie said. "So exciting to watch rehearsals and see the play come to life."

"I hope that when everyone is in costume and the rooms are decorated, it will all take them back to Victorian London. I never would have pulled this off without you and Mary Ann."

"Did I hear my name?" Mary Ann called, coming into the kitchen.

"Say, I love the posters in the rotunda. Glad they arrived in time." She poured herself a cup of coffee.

"If you dim the lights," Sadie said, "it'll be good and creepy."

"I hope so. I wanted to create an eerie, Jack the Ripper feel. Did you notice the copy of the old newspaper headlining the famous Whitechapel murders?"

"Yes," Mary Ann said, "but my favorites are the posters of The George & Vulture pub and The Blind Beggar pub."

"You should have heard some of the other names," Liz said. "How does The Slug and Lettuce grab you?"

Mary Ann burst out laughing. "The Slug and Lettuce? Ugh." She shook her head, her beautiful silver hair swinging in its long bob. "This mystery weekend should be such fun."

Liz agreed. After the six guests arrived, Liz would give them instructions and divide them up into three Sherlock Holmes/John Watson pairs. After supper, Act One of the weekend mystery would be presented in the dining room.

Beans, Liz's—or, rather, the inn's—English bulldog, waddled into the kitchen and slurped noisily from his water bowl, splattering the floor all around it. Then he stood by Liz at the stove, leaning his heavy weight against her leg. "Your kibble's over there, Beans," she said. "This bubble and squeak is for the guests."

While leftover roast beef and vegetables mashed together and fried in patties was certainly authentic, Liz thought she'd have to be awfully hungry to eat that for breakfast. But there were no scones and clotted cream for the average Londoner during Sherlock Holmes' time.

"Jackson liked this dish," she continued, "so maybe my guests will too." Jackson Cross, the town's handsome mayor, had been her taste tester, and he'd loved the samples.

"And I loved the porridge," Sadie said. "The treacle syrup reminded me of eating blackstrap molasses at my grandmother's." She peered into the window of the oven. "Your biscuits don't seem old-time London to me though."

"They're not. Those are my last practice for the bed-and-breakfast reviewer coming on Monday. He wants a total Amish experience." She pushed Drew Garrett's letter across the counter to her friends to read while she took out the biscuits. She gently nudged Beans aside with her foot. "I know it's warmer in here," she told the dog, "but the oven is not your personal furnace."

Beans gave Liz an offended look and trotted into the utility room. Liz heard him drop like a stone onto the floor. He was probably asleep already.

"What an exciting opportunity!" Mary Ann said, waving the letter.

"I agree." Liz slid the biscuits onto the rack for cooling. "I wish he hadn't insisted on coming this Monday though. Having even one day between the mystery guests leaving and his arrival would have given me some breathing room." She set the baking sheet in the sink. "But he said it was the only time available in his schedule, so it can't be helped."

The reviewer's letter explained that he was writing a book on B&Bs around the country, separating the establishments into rugged, historic, coastal, Old West, Southern plantation, and country lifestyle categories. His book would include photos of the inn, its most popular recipes, and his review.

Mary Ann glanced up. "You've been serving authentic Amish baked goods since you opened the inn. You don't need to practice."

Liz smoothed the front of her apron. "Maybe not, but the idea of having a professional reviewer judging every bite of my cooking makes me a bit nervous."

"What else will you be serving him?" Sadie asked, sorting through the recipe cards on Liz's kitchen desk.

"Brown sugar oatmeal pancakes and pumpkin custard pie."

Liz's small workstation was snowed under with Amish recipes and grocery lists, notes about costumes and props, plus the name and address of each mystery weekend guest. On top was an envelope from the bank. Every Friday she paid Sarah Borkholder, a young Amish woman who helped at the inn and wanted her wages in cash. Whipping around, Sadie knocked the stack of papers to the floor.

"Sorry, Liz."

"Don't worry about it," Liz said, scooping it all up and stuffing the papers into a drawer. "I've made a mess in here. Too much to do and too little time. And like I said, I'm a bit nervous."

Sadie plopped herself down on one of the stools at the island. "It's not like you to be nervous about your cooking."

"I know, but there's a lot riding on Mr. Garrett's visit. He could potentially really help—or hurt—my business. Inclusion in his B&B book would be a big deal. But first, his review will appear in a national travel magazine. I've decided to put him in the Amish Room, fill him with authentic Amish food, and escort him to see some of the local Amish farms and stores."

"Have him pop into the fabric shop too," Mary Ann suggested. "We have an Amish doll display up now."

"I will. I want his experience to be truly memorable." Liz took off her apron and hung it on the pantry hook. "I'm sorry to run out on you, but I have to head out to pick up the costumes."

"But your kitchen's a disaster," Sadie said.

Liz laughed. "You're right. It is." Her counters were cluttered with food-encrusted bowls and wooden spoons, and grease splatters dotted her stove.

"Want some help?" Mary Ann asked.

"No, you have your shop to run. And Sarah's coming in to hold down the fort while I run errands. I'll help her clean up when I get back." She peeked out the window. "Actually, she should be here by now."

Liz hated this last-minute rushing. The outfits should have arrived at the costume store yesterday. The rentals had also been more expensive than she'd bargained on. Thankfully she'd been able to borrow some props and partial outfits from the Pleasant Creek Playhouse. She'd considered asking the Material Girls—their quilting group that met weekly at Sew Welcome—to make outfits for her, but she needed too many.

"What are you picking up?" Mary Ann asked.

"We'll have three Sherlocks in cloaks and deerstalker hats, each with a black clay pipe, collecting clues around the inn. And we'll have three Watson sidekicks."

"How do you know their costumes will fit?"

"I asked for their sizes when they signed up, then ordered them a bit bigger, just in case. If the jackets are too tight, they don't have to be buttoned." Liz poured coffee into an insulated mug to take with her. "The Watson characters wear looser jackets anyway, and they should fit anyone."

Mary Ann raised an eyebrow. "Are you dressing up too? Did you rent a costume for yourself?"

"I wanted to, but it was a bit pricey, and I couldn't find anything at the playhouse either," Liz said. "I just plan to wear a long skirt and lacy blouse with a high collar. I did find a pattern for a Victorian skirt that I wanted to make, plus a blouse with leg-of-mutton sleeves, but I ran out of time to sew anything that complicated."

Packing away the bubble and squeak in the refrigerator, Liz stared at an empty space on the lower shelf where she usually kept Beans's favorite treat. Was she out of bologna already? She'd bought some to make sure he didn't pester the guests all weekend for extra food.

At least, she'd meant to.

"Let's see what you're wearing," Sadie said.

Liz turned, and wondered at the meaningful glance that passed between her two friends. "Sure, but I only have a minute." Liz motioned for them to follow her to her private quarters off the kitchen where the skirt and blouse were draped over the back of her small couch. On her desk was a pattern she'd found. "This is what I had in mind originally. And here are the Victorian-style earrings I found." She held one up for them to see. A delicate freshwater pearl dangled from a hand-carved cameo made from a beige shell.

"Lovely." Mary Ann admired them, then bent over the dress pattern. "They really went in for the hourglass figure then, didn't they? And get a look at these sleeves."

"Like balloon biceps," Sadie added, picking up the skirt. With the skirt in one hand and her coffee mug in the other, she did a small spin about the room, hugging the skirt to her waist as it whirled out around her.

"Look out!" Mary Ann cried as Sadie's foot caught the edge of Liz's rocker.

Sadie's coffee slopped over the side of her mug as she lurched to keep her balance. The liquid ran down the front of Liz's skirt.

"Oh no." Mary Ann looked aghast.

Just what Liz needed—one more thing to do before the guests arrived. She chided herself at the thought. It had been an accident.

"I'm so sorry." Sadie brushed at the skirt with little effect. The coffee didn't show much on the navy blue, but the lighter blue lacy inserts were stained dark brown.

"Give it to me," Mary Ann said. "We'll get it cleaned and pressed before your guests arrive. I promise."

"Thank you. If I'm ready when they get here, it'll be a small miracle." Liz took a deep breath. "My bigger concern is impressing that reviewer on Monday."

Sadie rolled her eyes. "With everything else going on, I don't see how—"

Mary Ann cut in smoothly. "He'll be wowed. You'll be more than ready for him."

Liz forced a smile. "I plan to be." But secretly she had the same reservations Sadie had begun to voice. *Have I bitten off more than I can chew?*

At the sound of the front door opening, Mary Ann and Sadie waved and left. Their footsteps echoed across the rotunda as they hurried to open their Sew Welcome Shop.

Turning, Liz's glance fell on the package propped by the door that she needed to post. She'd mail it to her godson, Steve, on the way to collect the costumes. At least the small Pleasant Creek Post Office was never busy. It would only take five extra minutes.

A few minutes later, bundled up against the cold, Liz left through the utility room, stepping over the immense lump snoring on the rug. She leaned down and sniffed, then grinned. Bologna breath. So that's where the lunch meat had gone. At least she wasn't losing her memory. But how had Beans managed to swipe it before she closed the fridge door?

Shaking her head, Liz cradled the package for her godson in her arms and pulled the back door closed. She climbed into her black Acura. Steam puffed from her mouth as she started the car and pulled around the side of the inn. Since it was only two blocks to the Pleasant Creek Post Office, there'd be no time for the car to warm up.

Parking in front of the post office, Liz pushed up her coat sleeve and glanced at her watch. At least it wasn't the Christmas rush yet, so the line at the post office should be short. But she'd need to fill out an overseas slip, which would take extra time. While her godson wasn't in the thick of the fighting right now, he was still stationed abroad. She tried to send him care packages every few weeks. It helped her to feel as if she was doing something important since she couldn't be with him.

Right now, in the cold climate, Steve wanted instant hot cocoa, energy bars, packs of peanuts and almonds, foot powder, stocking caps, and disposable hand warmers. He always said he loved the reminders from home. Liz knew her godson's mother would have gladly done the same if she were still alive.

She got out of the car and hurried inside. She loved the historic little post office with its original stained glass signs over each window: *Money Order*, *Registry*, and *General Delivery*. To the side were brass drops for letters and packages.

There was no line, and in five minutes Liz had mailed the package. If the rest of the morning went this smoothly, she might have a fighting chance of being ready when her guests arrived after all. Head down and fishing in her bag for her keys, Liz pushed on the glass door. At the same time, it opened wide, and she stumbled out.

"Sorry!" A hand grabbed her arm and stopped her fall. "Hi, Liz."

"David, hi," Liz said, pushing her bag back up on her shoulder. "I didn't even see you."

David Mills—a tall, thin man in his thirties—had moved to Pleasant Creek two months before. He worked in food services at a nearby hospital and went to her church.

He released her elbow. "Looked like you were a million miles away."

Liz nodded. "Got a lot on my mind today. How are you?"

"Good, good." His mouth was wide and straight, turning lopsided when he smiled. "Will you be at the church's craft show this weekend? I suppose your sewing group is raffling another quilt."

"Yes, we are." Liz turned her back to the wind. "I won't be at the craft show myself though. I'm having a Sherlock Holmes mystery weekend. I have six guests coming today who will try to solve a crime."

"A crime?" A shadow passed over David's sharply angled face so briefly that Liz wondered if she'd really seen it. "Should be fun."

"I hope so. I'm off to pick up some costumes I ordered." Liz took a step toward her car. "You have a good weekend."

"I will." He followed her and opened the door for her. He hit the remote button on his key fob and Liz heard the *snick* of a lock opening on the vehicle right next to hers. "I'll be entertaining in the children's ward with some magic tricks."

"You're a magician?"

"Amateur only." That same troubled shadow passed over his face and disappeared. If Liz hadn't been so short on time, she would have asked about the kinds of tricks he did. And if there was anything wrong.

"I'd like to talk longer, but I have to run if I'm to be ready when my guests show up."

With a smile that failed to reach his eyes, David stepped back. "Sorry for keeping you talking in this cold."

"No problem. Good luck with your magic show." Liz got into her car and headed out of town.

———————

A short time later, Liz pulled into a parking place across the street from Costume Craze. Inside the brightly lit shop, Liz encountered mannequins dressed as characters from a popular science fiction movie. On her right, Dorothy and Toto faced off with the Wicked Witch of the West.

Just ahead, a young woman sat behind a counter, her mouth holding three straight pins. A scarlet silk skirt was spread in front of her, revealing a rip half repaired.

"Help you?" she mumbled around the pins.

"I'm Liz Eckardt. I have three Sherlock Holmes costumes and three Dr. Watson costumes to pick up."

"Right." She removed the pins from her mouth and stuck them in the pincushion on her wrist, then disappeared through a swinging door. In two minutes she was back, pushing a rolling rack that held six zippered plastic bags. "Here you go." She read off the sizes from a list. "Correct?"

"Yes," Liz said, hoping each of her guests had been honest.

The girl unzipped one of the bags to reveal its contents. She laid a Sherlock cape and deerstalker hat on the counter, then handed Liz a black plastic curved pipe that went with it. She unzipped a second bag. "Here's a John Watson ensemble."

Liz grinned. "They look even more authentic than the pictures on the website."

"Please warn people to be careful." The girl lifted the silk skirt. "Too many costumes come back looking like this. I have to charge to mend them."

"I'll tell them." *Rental is expensive enough without repair fees.*

Liz signed the contract and gave the clerk her credit card, and then the two of them rolled the rack out the door and across the street. They laid the costume bags flat in the back seat of the car.

After she checked her to-do list, Liz leaned back against the headrest and took three slow, deep breaths. "It's going to be great," she told herself firmly. "I'm ready for this."

Shivering, she turned up the car's heat. At that moment, her phone rang. The screen said *Brian Culpepper*, an acquaintance who was playing a doctor in the mystery scenes this weekend.

"Brian, hi," she said. "It's almost showtime. I picked up your costume and a doctor's bag at the playhouse the other day."

His only response was a hacking cough. "Sorry, Liz," he finally said, his voice raspy.

Oh, please no. "Are you all right? You don't sound good."

"I put off calling you till I saw the doctor this morning," he said, coughing again. "I have laryngitis."

"That's awful," Liz said, feeling both concern and a rising panic. "Are you gargling? Did the doctor give you something for it?"

"Antibiotics. Apparently I have some bacterial infection."

"You mean it's contagious?"

"Yes, at least while I've got a fever. I'm sorry, but I won't be able to do the mystery weekend. I feel rotten leaving you in the lurch like this."

"Don't worry about that," Liz said. "Your health is much more important. I'll figure something out."

"The doctor isn't in Act One or Two, remember. Hopefully you can find a substitute by tomorrow afternoon for Act Three."

"I'm sure I'll find someone. You just get better."

When she hung up, Liz caught a glimpse of her creased forehead in the rearview mirror. She hadn't wanted Brian to feel any worse than he already did, and she knew it wasn't his fault, but she honestly had no idea how to replace him on such short notice.

And even if she found someone, could he learn his lines and find time to practice with the other actors in just over twenty-four hours? She couldn't imagine how.

2

On the way back to the inn, Liz barely noticed the streets she passed as she focused on replacing an actor *today*.

At an intersection, she looked both ways. To her left, a block away, an ambulance turned into the emergency entrance of the town's hospital. She started to pull out to turn right, but on an impulse, she hit the brakes.

David Mills, the man she'd run into at the post office, worked at that hospital. Would *he* be willing to play the doctor in two scenes for her mystery weekend? It wouldn't take much of his time, and there were only a few lines.

He'd called himself an amateur magician. He performed for kids, so maybe he could act in her mystery play. Her thoughts whirled from one idea to another as possibilities occurred to her. Could he add something even more special to the mystery weekend?

As a magician, David would have sleight-of-hand skills. Pickpockets had roamed the streets of Victorian London, using their own form of sleight of hand. David would be perfect, if she could convince him to replace her sick friend as the doctor, and also to act as a pickpocket.

But what about the costume? David was considerably taller than Brian. However, both were very slender. Surely David could make it work.

A loud honk behind Liz jolted her out of her reverie. She turned left and headed to the hospital to see if David was at work yet.

Liz found him in the cafeteria, filling the huge salad bar in preparation for the lunch crowd. He jerked when she touched his arm.

"Hi," he said. "I never expected to see you twice in one day. Are you visiting someone?"

"Yes. You." Liz motioned for him to keep spooning the three-bean salad into the stainless steel serving bowl. "I want to ask you a big, big favor."

He raised one eyebrow. "Ask away."

She explained about Brian. "He was supposed to play the part of the doctor this weekend. The doctor's only in two scenes, one on Saturday afternoon and one Sunday afternoon." She mentally crossed her fingers. "Could you do this for me?"

"Me? Act?" David shook his head so hard he looked in danger of snapping his neck. "That's not me. Not at all."

"But isn't performing magic tricks for an audience like acting?"

"That's different. I'm going bed to bed to do tricks for the sickest children, one at a time. I don't perform in front of groups." He shook his head again. "I appreciate being asked, but I can't. I have zero acting experience."

"But I wanted to use your magician skills as well," Liz said. "You'd add a lot to the weekend if you'd also be my mystery pickpocket. It would involve the guests and give them the full flavor of the streets of Victorian London." She sensed David softening a bit and laid a hand on his arm. "You must be good at sleight of hand if you're a magician, and that's the only skill a good pickpocket needs. Right?"

"Well," David said doubtfully, "it's true that pickpockets have to be masters of diversion. They focus attention elsewhere while sliding a hand into someone's pocket."

"Exactly."

"How many lines would I have to memorize?"

"Just a few. Honest."

"Well, okay," he said reluctantly. "I'll give it my best shot."

"Thank you so much. You can pick up your costume tonight or in the morning." She felt like a weight had been lifted from her. "I'll give you a script when you pick up your costume."

"Sure." David already looked as if he regretted his decision, so Liz gave him a bright smile before she left.

Liz would have felt better if David had showed some confidence. Between his job and doing magic tricks for sick children, she knew he wouldn't have much time to learn his lines, and he'd have no time to rehearse with the others. She might have to ask Mary Ann to hide somewhere out of sight and be his prompter so he wouldn't have to read from his script.

Dodging the icy spots, she sprinted across the hospital parking lot. *I'll cross that bridge when I come to it.*

———————— ⁓⁓⁓⁓⁓ ————————

Liz wiped the mascara smudges from under her eyes and reapplied a dab of lipstick. The clock on her bathroom counter ticked relentlessly. It was already two thirty, and the guests were scheduled to arrive between three and three thirty.

Liz grabbed some black slacks and a maroon cable-knit sweater, wishing that her planned Victorian skirt and blouse were available. Hopefully she'd have them back by tonight. Her vision of greeting her guests in Victorian clothing, framed by the London posters in the rotunda, had gone up in smoke. *Oh well.* The guests weren't paying to view her outfit. They were coming to play detective, and she was determined to make them feel welcome.

She was just smoothing her hair when a robust voice called, "Yoo-hoo! Anyone here?"

Liz ran her fingers through her hair, hoping the cheery-sounding person was looking for Sew Welcome. But the second greeting sounded even closer. Liz put on her shoes and left to meet the owner of the voice, whom she found in the kitchen.

"Hello," she said, wondering how long the woman had been there. "I'm Liz."

"Of course you are." The woman's voice was so nasal she sounded as if she had a clothespin on her nose. She dropped her soft-sided duffel bag, its pattern made of rows of books, and pulled off her boots. "I'm Vivian Farley, but my friends call me Viv." She replaced the boots with a pair of black sparkly ballet flats with bows.

"Welcome to—"

"I love your granite counters and all these shiny appliances. You must not have grandchildren around. No little fingerprints." She peered over a pair of half-glasses worn low on her nose. "And a copper teakettle. How homey."

Liz jumped in when her guest was forced to take a breath. "It's so nice to meet you, Vivian—Viv," she amended. "Let's go to—"

"Where are my manners?" Viv leaned forward, grasping Liz's right hand between her own hands and squeezing.

"We'll go into the sitting room and wait for the others to arrive." She stooped to grab Vivian's bag. "I'll put this at the bottom of the staircase for now."

Liz led Vivian to the sitting room. A cheery fire crackled in the fireplace, giving the couch and chairs a burnished glow. Liz always felt herself relax when stepping into this room.

"Where's everyone else?" Viv asked.

"It's not quite three o'clock yet, but I imagine they'll arrive soon."

"I'm the president of my mystery book club, so I want to be paired up this weekend with another mystery reader."

Liz smiled. "I'm guessing that most people who signed up for a Sherlock weekend fit that description. I'll let everyone introduce themselves when they arrive."

She'd barely spoken when the front door opened and closed with a jarring bang. Liz winced, hoping that the glass in the door hadn't cracked. She hurried out to the foyer. "Hello!"

Standing in her foyer was a short, heavy man wearing a mashed-down felt hat. His coat hung open, and his round stomach bulged beneath a plaid vest. When he caught sight of Liz, he whipped off his hat. A thick shock of brown hair fell across one eye, giving him the look of a wise old lion. He whipped out a comb and ran it through his hair.

"Please come in where it's warm. I'm Liz."

"Pleasure." He nodded, then pushed his hair back again. "Paul Levine."

He dropped his luggage—made of scarred leather that looked as if it had been through a war—at the foot of the staircase next to Viv's book duffel. He shrugged off his coat, folded it, and laid it across his suitcase. Then he hitched up his pants, but his cuffs still drooped at the ankles.

Liz led him into the sitting room. "Vivian Farley, meet Paul Levine," she said.

"Hi, Paul," Vivian said. "Won't this be a fun weekend? I can't wait. I'm the president of my town's mystery book club, so I think I'll be a shoo-in for this." She peered at him over the top of her half glasses. "What do you do for a living?"

"I'm retired." He pulled up a chair that suddenly seemed very small and sat on it, spilling over on both sides.

"Retired from what?" Vivian asked.

Before he could answer, the front door opened again. "I'll be right back," Liz said. "Go ahead and get acquainted." She caught a glimpse of Paul's pained expression, but Liz couldn't help that. At least Vivian was friendly and enthusiastic. Hopefully she would pair up with someone who appreciated her personality.

"Hello, come in." Liz held the door for a taller man about her own age, his eyes deep-set under heavy brows.

"Is this the mystery game place?" His eyebrows dipped into a scowl, spoiling his otherwise handsome looks.

"Yes, this is the Olde Mansion Inn. You must be—"

"Jeremy Nichols." He puffed out his cheeks with a slight, self-satisfied smile, like a preening cockatoo. He paused, as if waiting for Liz to exclaim something.

"I'm glad to meet you. Two of the other mystery weekend guests just arrived." She pointed to the small pile of luggage. "You can leave your things there for now."

He propped what appeared to be an oversize briefcase by the stairs and followed her into the sitting room. There Vivian was giving a monologue on her favorite mystery writers to the trapped-looking rotund retiree.

"Let me introduce our third guest," Liz interrupted. She motioned to the man who'd stopped in the doorway to survey his surroundings. "Jeremy Nichols, this is—"

"Jeremy Nichols?" Vivian practically screamed. "The mystery writer?"

Liz turned in surprise. "Is that right?"

Jeremy made an effort to look humble, but totally failed. "Yes, but I promise not to take unfair advantage. If I solve the mystery before anyone else, it'll only be beginner's luck." He dug into his jeans pocket and pulled out a gold coin. "And because of this good-luck piece. I'm never without it."

Practically hyperventilating, Vivian patted the couch beside her. "Sit here, Jeremy. Do you mind if I call you Jeremy? We have *so* much in common. My book club discussed your books *The Crooked Man* and *The Empty House* two years ago. They were absolutely thrilling!"

"Thank you." His short-clipped mustache resembled a twitching toothbrush.

"You haven't had a new release in a long time. Why not?"

Jeremy's eyebrows dipped in another scowl. "I was burned out for a while—promoting with book tours and TV interviews takes a lot out of you—but this weekend might give me some inspiration." He took a seat by Vivian and rapped his knuckles on the end table. "Knock on wood."

Liz interrupted. "When everyone arrives, we'll draw names. Then each pair can decide who will play Sherlock and who will be Watson."

"We *have* to be partners!" Vivian gripped Jeremy's arm so tightly that he winced. "We're the perfect pair to solve the crime this weekend." She turned to Liz, her eyes almost feverish. "List us as one of the Holmes and Watson teams."

"We'll pair up after everyone arrives," Liz said, "and it shouldn't be long now." She paused and listened. "Sounds like another car just pulled into the drive. Excuse me."

When she stepped out onto the front porch, two ladies were already making their way slowly up the sidewalk. Liz hugged herself, noting how the wind had picked up. She hoped it didn't blow the thin older lady right off her tiny feet.

This must be the mother-daughter pair she was expecting. "Mrs. Rollins?" she asked. "Welcome to the Olde Mansion Inn. And you too, Miss Rollins."

"Call me Penny," the younger woman said, setting down the matching set of floral suitcases. "This is my mother, Louise."

"Come in out of the cold." Liz held the door and took Louise's arm, noting her thin frame even through the fabric of her coat sleeve.

Her hair was mostly gray, with braids wound into a crown on top of her head. Strands of silver were threaded through the braids like tinsel. Louise twisted her fingers together nervously.

Her daughter couldn't have been more of a contrast. Penny's fuzzy, graying hair was pulled back in a single fat braid. Her face, with its pale powder, had the soft look of a marshmallow. Her mouth settled in an unhappy droop.

But then Beans appeared in the rotunda, and Penny's face lit up. She dropped to her knees and hugged his sturdy neck. "I love bulldogs," she said. "What's his name?"

"Beans."

The bulldog gazed up at Liz as if expecting her to disentangle him from this stranger.

"Where did you get him?"

"Actually, Beans came with the inn when I bought it. Do you have a bulldog yourself?"

"No, but I love to play with the animals at the Humane Society where I volunteer."

Louise pointed a long skeletal finger. "Does he bark?" she asked faintly.

Liz patted his head. "He's usually too busy sleeping. He's not much of a watchdog, I'm afraid. It would take too much energy."

Beans had his own strict schedule, largely based on his stomach, whether it needed food, belly rubs, or his soft rug to rest on. As soon as Penny loosened her grip, Beans slunk away without making a sound.

"I'm afraid Mother can't stand barking."

"I can't?" Louise asked, frowning.

Penny gave Liz a wan smile and then helped her mother off with her tweed coat, adjusting the fringed shawl she wore underneath. Louise's arms were little more than bones fleshed out with skin as thin as tissue paper. She clutched her shawl tightly around herself and shivered delicately.

"Come this way and you can meet the others. We're waiting for one last person to arrive."

Liz led the way to the sitting room, but Penny pulled back on her arm.

"Yes?" asked Liz.

"I just wanted to say one thing. Well, two things really." She lowered her voice to a whisper, and a tiny tic flickered at the edge of her right eyelid. "Mother will only play the mystery game if she is partnered with me."

"Are you sure? You both might enjoy getting better acquainted with the other guests."

"No. Mother doesn't mix well with strangers. The other thing. . ."

"Yes?"

"This weekend we're celebrating Mother's recovery after some recent heart surgery." She lowered her voice even more. "It just occurred to me that maybe you have something planned that would be too frightening for Mother's heart. Ghouls jumping out of the dark, skeletons in cemeteries, things like that?"

Liz smiled. "No worries on that score. Not at all. You'll see why when I explain to the group how the weekend is set up."

Penny visibly relaxed. "Thank you. I'm much relieved." She took her mother's arm. "Let's go meet the others," she said.

In the sitting room the mystery writer and the book club president were in an animated discussion about mystery authors, talking over each other much of the time. The retired man ignored them and flipped through a magazine. Liz thought he looked decidedly unhealthy, but maybe it was only the winter pallor people often acquired this time of year.

After introducing Penny and Louise Rollins, Liz steered the shivering Louise to a chair near the fireplace. She'd need to make sure Louise had access to plenty of coffee, tea, and hot chocolate.

By three forty-five, even Liz was tired of the Vivian-Jeremy domination of the conversation. She considered giving her instructions for the weekend, but she didn't want to repeat everything when the last guest arrived, and they couldn't pair off until everyone was there. The sixth guest was Cherise Tulette, an up-and-coming movie starlet. She wasn't a full-blown star yet, but Liz had seen her in two movies where she'd done a creditable job in her supporting roles. Liz was curious how she'd ended up in Indiana and why she'd chosen the mystery weekend.

Who knows? Maybe someday I'll be able to say I knew her before she was famous when she stayed at my inn.

Just then, the front door in the foyer opened and slammed shut. Liz hadn't heard another car pull in, so it might be a walk-in for Sew Welcome. She jumped up to go and check at the same time a shrill voice rang out.

"I'm here now!" Heels clicked across the rotunda. Then Cherise Tulette stood in the doorway of the sitting room. Well, not exactly stood, Liz decided. *Leaned* was a more apt expression. Or *draped*.

"I'm here, so let the games begin." She tossed her blonde hair from one side to the other like a horse's mane. Liz half-expected her to neigh or paw the ground with her slender foot.

"Do come in. We're glad you made it."

"You have such a beautiful place," she said. "Like a movie setting for one of the old classics where actresses sweep down circular staircases in gowns and mink coats." Her voice was smooth and sweet as honey, reminding Liz of one of the roles she'd seen Cherise play. However, her eyes, framed by thin arched eyebrows and a layer of false lashes, glittered like sharp stones.

Jeremy jumped to his feet to welcome her, and Vivian glared daggers at the new arrival. Paul barely glanced at her and made no effort to stand.

Liz pointed to a second chair near the fireplace and made the introductions. Only two guests—Jeremy and Viv—recognized Cherise's name. Cherise left a perfumed trail as she entered the room.

Viv piped up brightly. "We were just pairing off," she said. "I'm a mystery book club president, so it's only natural that I would be a team with the mystery writer." She gripped Jeremy's shirt sleeve.

"And this is my mother, Louise," Penny said. "We'll be another team."

"I had planned to draw names to choose teammates—"

Louise appeared alarmed and grabbed her daughter's arm. Penny patted her hand. "It's all right, Mother. I already explained to her why you and I will be partners."

"And we're a team too," Vivian insisted. "We've already been discussing our strategy for the weekend."

Liz decided this was a battle not to fight. "Well, that makes it simple then."

Paul was listening with his eyes half closed. Then suddenly he leaned forward, distaste clear on his face at the realization that he was going to be paired up with the movie starlet.

"Now that we're all here, we need to deal with some housekeeping details. I'll bring in some snacks. Help yourself to whatever flavor coffee you'd like." She pointed to the single-cup coffeemaker in the corner. "Then I'll run over the schedule for the mystery weekend. I'll also hand out the keys to your rooms so that you can get settled. There's no elevator, so tell me if any of you need help with your bags." Liz headed to the kitchen.

"Shall I help with the refreshments?" Cherise offered.

"I'm fine, thanks. I'll be just a second."

She hurried off to the kitchen, hoping the group jelled better as the game got underway. As she loaded the cookies and other snacks onto a little rolling table, Liz gazed in gratitude around her sparkling kitchen. Sarah Borkholder was worth her weight in gold. In fact, maybe Liz would add a bonus to this week's wages. She took an extra bill from her petty cash, which was stashed in an antique sugar bowl, then reached into the top drawer of the desk for the bank envelope.

Only it wasn't there.

Liz stood there, puzzled. How had the money disappeared? Sarah never helped herself to the money envelope. And yet, no one else had been around except the Sew Welcome ladies.

And Vivian. Liz had a sudden image of Vivian standing in her kitchen when Liz had come out of her private quarters. Vivian had said she'd just arrived, but had she? Or had she explored the kitchen before making her presence known, while Liz was putting on her makeup?

Liz shut the drawer at the sound of sharp heels clicking on her tiled floor.

Cherise hurried to Liz's side, her breathy stage whisper not two inches from her ear. "I know I arrived later than everyone else, but it wasn't my fault. My driver couldn't find your place."

"Not a problem," Liz assured her. Liz highly suspected that the starlet had arrived late on purpose. Any actress knew that an effective entrance meant waiting for the largest audience possible.

"I knew you'd understand."

"Really, it's no problem." Liz moved away from Cherise so she could roll the coffee trolley.

Cherise stepped in front of the cart. "Since it's not my fault that I arrived last, I shouldn't be penalized by being stuck with . . . that man." She waited for agreement, but Liz just stared at her. "I mean, I can see why the Gruesome Twosome want to stick together—that old woman looks like a cadaver—but otherwise I think the pairing should be left up to everyone." She smirked, and Liz read her mind clearly. Cherise was implying that Jeremy would choose her over the clinging Vivian. She was probably right, but Liz didn't intend to get in the middle of it.

Liz chose her words carefully. "The other guests visited for forty-five minutes and discovered commonalities that made natural pairings. But if you want to ask them to reshuffle, you're welcome to do so."

Cherise bit her lower lip, then suddenly gave a blinding porcelain smile. Liz blinked. Cherise's expensive-looking teeth couldn't possibly be natural. They were too even, and the color was way too white.

"Well, it can't be helped then," Cherise said. "By the way, when I sent my confirmation, did I mention that I have a role in a new movie where I play the owner of a bed-and-breakfast?" She waited expectantly.

"Uh, that should be fun," Liz finally said. "If you have any questions this weekend—"

"I thought I'd shadow you to observe the real life of a B&B owner."

Liz willed herself not to let her feelings show. The last thing she needed this weekend was to be Cherise's tutor on the life of an innkeeper.

Back in the sitting room, Liz gave Vivian a sidelong glance. Had she taken Sarah's wage envelope? Was there any way to find out short of asking to search her purse? Liz helped everyone to hot drinks and ignored the retired man's plaintive expression, the mystery writer's annoyance at being trapped by Viv, and Cherise's narcissism.

Well, aren't we a happy group? Liz took a deep breath. As Cherise had said earlier, let the games begin.

3

All the guests except Cherise gathered around the trolley and helped themselves to the mouthwatering selection of cookies from the Sweet Everything bakery next door. Usually Liz made cookies for her guests herself, but she hadn't had time today. Cherise reclined on the couch after giving Liz exact instructions on how she liked her coffee. Liz served her, wondering if Cherise was taking notes for her innkeeper role.

By the time they were resettled, Liz was ready to outline the weekend.

"Before I hand out the costumes, let me give you the overview of the weekend." She handed each guest a gray folder with a black silhouette of Sherlock Holmes on the cover. "The first page of the handout is the schedule for the weekend." She waited while everyone but Louise found the schedule. Penny found hers and leaned close to her mother so they could share it.

Liz held up her copy. "The mystery you will solve is broken down into five acts. Some friends of mine have agreed to act them out to show you the crime, the clues, and the suspects. You even have special Sherlock Holmes notepads in your folders for writing down clues."

"When do we see Act One?" Cherise asked.

"The first act will be performed tonight at seven o'clock in the dining room." She held up a second sheet. "If you look at the blue paper, you'll find a list of places to eat that are close by, within walking distance if you bundle up." Papers rustled as they found their lists.

Paul folded his hands over his stomach and frowned. "I'm not keen to walk anywhere. Does the pizza place deliver?"

"Yes, I believe it does," Liz said, "and you can certainly do that. But for supper tonight, the dining room is off-limits. It's been decorated to look like a Victorian dining room. You're welcome to eat in the kitchen though. We have lots of space."

"No, I'll eat in my room."

Liz inwardly groaned. The last guest who'd ordered pizza had eaten it in bed and made a huge mess. She'd had to have the bed quilt professionally cleaned.

Cherise shot daggers at her partner in crime. Jeremy spoke up then. "Cherise is more than welcome to join us for dinner tonight."

Cherise smirked at Vivian as she thanked them both for the invitation. Vivian's expression clearly said it wasn't *her* idea.

"One last thing," Liz said. "In your folder is a yellow sheet, a list of sights you might enjoy visiting in your spare time, along with directions. As you know, we're in the heart of Amish country. Even in November, their farm craft stores are open for business all day Saturday."

"What if we don't want to walk?" Vivian asked. "It'll be pretty cold after dark." She glanced at Jeremy, but frowned when she saw Jeremy's eyes were on Cherise.

"You're free to drive if you like," Liz said. "If you parked in the inn's driveway, you might want to repark out on the street to avoid being boxed in by cars behind you."

Liz handed out the keys to their rooms. "Penny and Louise have the two rooms on the top floor, the Sunrise Room facing east and the Sunset Room facing west. You ladies will share the one bathroom on that floor. The rest of you will be on the second floor, where you will each have a private bath."

She gave Jeremy a key to the Amish Room at the top of the staircase. Vivian was given a key to the Heirloom Room next door to Jeremy's room, which seemed to please her. Cherise was in the Rose of Sharon Room on the other side of Vivian, and then Liz gave a key to Paul for the Somewhere in Time Room.

"Now, if you'll gather by the stairs and sort out your luggage, I'll get your costumes."

Liz ran through her mind the sizes of the costumes. Unless she missed her guess, only the heavyset Paul Levine had told the truth about his size. He was one of the largest Sherlock Holmeses in history.

Liz hurried to her private quarters for three of the costumes, then ran back for the other three. She stood beside the poster depicting the six famous Whitechapel murders.

"Paul, Jeremy, and Penny, you get the Sherlock capes, plus you'll each have a traditional deerstalker hat and curved pipe." She handed them around. "I'm afraid that John Watson's coat won't look nearly as impressive, but remember that Sherlock is nothing without his sidekick."

"Yeah, remember that," Vivian said coyly, nudging Jeremy. "We'll be an unbeatable team. Everyone else might as well concede right now."

Before Jeremy could respond, the outside door opened, a gust of wind rattling the window behind her. Penny and her mother startled and stared at the door. Liz glanced over her shoulder.

"Hi, David," She was grateful that he'd stopped by for his script and costume so soon. "Everyone," Liz called, "this is David Mills. He graciously agreed to pinch-hit this weekend because one of our actors came down with laryngitis." He bowed awkwardly. Liz glanced up at him, struck again by how tall and thin he was. She remembered Sadie once saying that he had to stand twice to make a shadow. "The script is on the kitchen counter. Through that door on the right."

Penny raised her hand. "What if it's too cold to take Mother out sightseeing much?"

"Since this is a Sherlock weekend," Liz said, grateful that she'd planned ahead, "I've put books on detection in the library and in your rooms, books like *Mastermind* and *The Sherlock Holmes Handbook*. We'll also have a viewing of *The Hound of the Baskervilles* tomorrow night for anyone who's interested. And there will be lots of time to get together with your teammate to decipher your clues." She grinned, eager to reveal her unique feature of the weekend. "One last thing. So that the inn will feel more like the dark streets of Victorian London, a pickpocket will move among us this weekend. Everything taken from you will be returned at the end of the weekend, or whenever you request it. There will be an extra prize for anyone who catches the pickpocket in the act."

"What fun!' Vivian exclaimed.

While the guests claimed their luggage from the pile in the rotunda and headed upstairs to settle in, Liz hurried to the kitchen. David was studying the script at the kitchen table.

"I highlighted the doctor's lines," Liz said. "There really aren't too many."

"I just wish I had more time to memorize them." David swung his legs around so he could face her. "I have something for you." From his back pocket he pulled a lacy handkerchief embroidered with purple pansies.

"This?" Liz asked, laughing.

"You told me to pick pockets and turn in the stuff to you."

"You picked a pocket already?" Liz laughed. "Let me guess. The older lady, Louise?"

"Easy pickings, actually," David admitted. "Ladies her age carry hankies tucked up their sleeves. The edge was hanging out, and when I bowed, I snatched it."

"I'll stick it in the safe, along with anything else you nab this weekend. This will add a real element of fun."

"Do you mind if I scout out the lay of the land?"

"No problem. You'll be in Acts Three and Five. Act Three will be the victim's bedroom, and we'll use the sitting room for that. Act Five will be in the victim's dining room. We'll use my dining room, with antique dishes and candelabra for a Victorian touch." She popped into her private quarters and returned carrying a coat with tails, complete with pocket watch on a chain, and a doctor's bag full of instruments. "The man you're replacing isn't as tall as you," she said, holding it up to him. "Will it fit?"

"It should, as long as the shoulders aren't too snug." He shrugged it on. Other than not hanging down as far as most tails did, it looked great.

"I can't thank you enough for doing this at such short notice. I hope it turns out to be fun for you too."

"I just hope I don't let your guests down or embarrass myself."

"You'll do fine," Liz assured him, hoping desperately that it was true.

He headed off to check out the dining room and sitting room. Soon Liz would need to finish decorations in the dining room so it would be ready for Act One that evening. She almost wished she didn't know the villain's identity or how he was going to commit the crime. She would have enjoyed playing along as a guest. Maybe, if it was a howling success, she'd make mystery weekends a regular thing. She might choose a warmer time of year if she did it again, although November worked well since it allowed for fires in all the fireplaces, which was authentic to the time period. Those Sherlock costumes would be mighty hot in August.

As Liz scanned her to-do list and detailed schedule for the weekend, she had the distinct feeling that she was being watched. Turning slowly, she caught movement in her peripheral vision. *Who needs help now?* She smiled, then turned to assist either Cherise, the budding innkeeper, or Penny, the worrywart daughter.

But no one was there.

At the same time, she heard the front door open and close. Poking her head into the rotunda, she spotted a customer entering the door of Sew Welcome. She could also make out David muttering in the dining room next door, rehearsing his lines.

Back in the kitchen, Liz heard the inn's front door open and close again. She was glad the shop was doing such a brisk business on a blustery Friday afternoon. Usually Saturday was their busiest day. She also heard footsteps on the staircase, probably a guest checking out the public rooms on the ground floor.

Just then, Sarah came inside, her cheeks red, and stamped her feet on the rug. "I'm finished now, Liz," she called. "I swept the snow off the porch and sidewalk."

Liz had completely forgotten the missing wage envelope. Where had it gone? Had she put it somewhere else in her rush to get ready for the guests? Or—and she hated to think this again—had someone taken it?

"Thank you, Sarah," Liz said, grabbing her coat from the hook by the back door. "I'll be right back with your week's pay."

By the time Liz had returned from the bank and paid Sarah, David had left and three of the guests were downstairs. From their friendly banter, it sounded like Cherise and Viv had buried the hatchet, at least until they made a decision about where to eat. Liz covered her smile as they each tried to out-charm each other to Jeremy. Admittedly he was better looking than the shambling retiree who'd ordered pizza to eat in his room, but what was Jeremy but a bragging writer who hadn't sold a new book in years, or so she'd heard?

Liz shook her head, chastising herself. It wasn't her place to judge her guests. She was there to serve them and ensure they had a fun getaway weekend.

She joined in with their discussion to answer questions about Mama's Home Cooking, which they could walk to, versus Pasta Heaven, the Italian restaurant on the north end of town, which would require driving. Liz relaxed as she listened to them make plans. Things would come together. They just needed to get past the uncomfortable phase of getting to know each other.

They were shrugging into their coats when footsteps clattered down the stairs. "No one go anywhere!" Penny called.

"We can wait," Vivian called upward. "Do you need more time to get ready?"

"No," Penny said, coming into view then. She carried a toiletries case by the handle, and it hung open. Reaching the ground floor, it took her half a minute to catch her breath. "When I was unpacking for Mother, I found this empty."

"What was in it?" Liz asked. She was used to guests leaving home without some necessities. "I keep extra amenities—hair dryers, soap, shampoo, mouthwash, and shower caps. What can I get for you?"

"You don't understand. I packed this case myself. It held some jewelry as well as her soaps and toothpaste. And it had her blood pressure medicine in it." She looked under the stairs as if expecting to find the spilled toiletries, but Liz could have told her that nothing was there.

Liz was at a loss. "Perhaps the case opened on your way here and spilled her things out in your car."

"I would have noticed," Penny said, near tears. "Mother needs her medication."

"We all sat in the sitting room for over an hour with our luggage piled out here before we got keys to our rooms," Vivian piped up. "People come in here off the street. Or was it your pickpocket? I don't think the pickpocketing should extend to our luggage, especially something important like medication."

"It doesn't," Liz assured her, keeping her voice even. "I'm sure it wasn't that." As best as she remembered, David had gone into the kitchen while they were in the sitting room, talking. But had they taken their luggage upstairs by the time he went to look at the dining room? "Surely it will all turn up. For now, let me get some extra things I keep on hand. And if you need her medicine tonight, have her doctor call her prescription to our local pharmacy. I'll get you the number."

Without waiting for an answer, Liz hurried to her private quarters. While she gathered a small basket of items and looked up the drugstore's phone number, she quickly called David. "Did you, by any chance, take anything from a guest's luggage in the hallway?"

"Absolutely not."

"I didn't think so, but I had to make sure you understood. One of the guests is missing something from her luggage. But I expect she'll find the things she's lost spilled out in her car."

She hung up and stood motionless, considering another alternative. Had someone she'd mistaken for a sewing shop customer helped herself to the contents of Louise's small toiletries case? Had the woman's jewelry caught a thief's eye? But if so, why not just take the jewelry and leave everything else? The theft might not have been noticed for hours that way.

Liz went back to the rotunda and joined the others. "Penny, is it possible that your mother misplaced the items in her room, maybe put them in the desk or nightstand?" She remembered how Louise had seemed confused when they arrived, asking her daughter if it was true that she didn't like barking dogs.

Penny puffed out her chest like a bantam rooster. "Come search our rooms, if you like," she said.

"I don't think that's necessary. I was just wondering if there was an explanation you hadn't thought of." Liz handed her the small wicker basket of toiletries and the drugstore phone number. "Please give your mother these things. And let me know if you want me to pick up something from the drugstore." She touched Penny's arm. "We'll find your things. I promise."

"How?" she demanded.

"I don't know at the moment," Liz said. "Would you like me to call the police? If the jewelry is valuable, we probably should."

The anger drained from Penny's face. "No, not yet anyway. I'll look through our things again."

Liz took a deep breath as she watched Penny, her back stiff, climb the stairs and disappear around the curve. When she was out of sight, Liz dashed out the back door to the parking area. It was possible, in carrying in the luggage and shepherding her mother into the inn, Penny hadn't noticed the case opening and the contents spilling out. Especially if her mother had been the one carrying the case.

She scoured the parking area and saw nothing out of place. After checking to make sure she wasn't being observed, Liz cupped her hands around her eyes and peered into the front and back seats of Penny's silver four-door. Nothing spilled there either. Liz sighed and headed back indoors.

Missing jewelry. Missing medication. Sarah's missing wages envelope. She'd wanted to build excitement for the weekend, but this had not been part of her plan.

What was going on here? Worry gnawed at the edges of Liz's mind. She hadn't meant to, but it appeared that she'd be investigating right along with her guests this weekend.

4

The closer it got to seven o'clock and the performance of Act One, the more excited Liz became. She was positive her guests would enjoy this. She hoped Penny had already discovered where her mother had mislaid her toiletries and jewelry. Mary Ann rushed in at six thirty with Liz's long skirt and lacy blouse clean and pressed. "I'm so sorry about this," she said again. "But you know Sadie."

Liz grinned. "Don't worry about it. They look good as new. Is Sadie with you?"

"She's chatting with your actors. We can't wait to see your opening scene." Mary Ann placed a hand over her heart. "And we solemnly promise to stay out of the way."

Liz grinned. She wasn't worried about Mary Ann, but she could easily imagine Sadie deciding to jump into the scene if she thought things needed livening up.

She went to her quarters to change. Now she could wear the earrings she'd bought for the weekend. She checked the back of her long skirt, making sure she wouldn't catch the hem with her heel. She was applying lipstick when she heard the outside door open, followed by laughing voices. She paused to listen. Yes, it was Jackson and Naomi, right on time.

After discovering that all the Pleasant Creek Playhouse actors were rehearsing for a major holiday production and couldn't help her, she'd been grateful when Jackson had agreed to play the starring role in her mystery performances. Jackson brought James Braithwaite, the wealthy Victorian collector, to life perfectly. The fact that he also possessed rugged good looks and an attractive smile didn't hurt, she admitted with a slight flutter of the heart. Jackson was the mayor of Pleasant Creek as well as the owner of Cross Furniture Company, which specialized in authentic, Amish-made wood furniture.

Naomi Mason was outgoing and friendly. Her personality made her bakery, Sweet Everything, a popular place. Since it was located next to the inn, Liz popped over there often, even if only for a cookie and a ten-minute break with her friend. Naomi was also a member of the Material Girls quilting group.

Liz tightened a wide belt over her skirt. No way would she ever wear the excruciatingly tight corsets she'd seen online. Dressing to impress only went so far.

She swept out to the kitchen, earrings swinging, and hoped she looked elegant. She *felt* elegant anyway, which was a change from her usual pants and sweater.

"Thanks for coming a bit early," she said, then stopped. "You both look terrific."

Jackson grinned and took a deep bow in tails, ruffled shirt, and trousers. "James Braithwaite, at your service. Please meet my comely wife."

Naomi curtsied, her lavender gown swaying.

"Twirl for us." Sadie took Naomi's hand and lifted it high. Naomi laughed as she spun around twice, her skirt ballooning out.

Liz glanced at the wall clock. "The guests will be down in a couple of minutes, so let's get ready in the dining room."

"Sadie and I can check on it for you," Mary Ann said. They disappeared into the adjoining room.

Liz glanced toward the foyer. "Did you happen to see Bert heading this way?"

Jackson shook his head. "Should I call him?"

Liz considered. "Yes, if you don't mind. He's never early, but he's also rarely late."

Bert Worth was Pleasant Creek's self-appointed historian with an office in the courthouse. Liz wondered how he would look as the butler with his full head of gray hair that fluffed around his head like a cloud. She hadn't had the nerve to ask him to cut it short for the weekend.

"Are you doing okay?" Naomi whispered. "Butterflies?"

Liz glanced around the rotunda, then pulled Naomi into the kitchen. "I'm nervous, but it's not because of the mystery weekend. Some things have disappeared in the last couple of hours."

"Disappeared? What things?"

"An envelope containing Sarah's wages. Some jewelry and medication that belongs to one of the guests." Liz frowned. "I'm not sure what to do. I expect I mislaid the money myself and it'll turn up. It's the jewelry and medication that worries me."

"Is it a police matter, do you think?"

"I offered to call them, but the guest declined." She glanced at the wall clock. "Time to go."

"Try not to worry."

Liz led the way next door to the dining room, enjoying the eerie mood of the shadowed rotunda with the London posters lit only by nearby candles. "As soon as Bert shows up, I'll bring in the guests."

"Did I hear my name?" Bert Worth blew in, along with a strong gust of wind.

Liz turned and her mouth dropped open. Sharply dressed in a black double-breasted tuxedo and white gloves, Bert stood at attention. And what had he done to his hair?

"I thought I'd better slick it back," he said, correctly interpreting her astonishment. "It's hair gel."

"It looks perfect," Naomi said.

"Very butler-like," Jackson added.

Liz grinned. "Quite handsome."

Bert nodded gravely, then laughed. "Glad you approve."

At that moment, a door above opened and closed. Liz motioned her friends to follow her. "The curtain is about to go up."

Outside the dining room she'd placed a sign that announced Act One. Inside, flames danced merrily in the fireplace, and two candelabra waited to be lit. Liz handed the lighter from the top drawer of the sideboard to Jackson. "Could you?" she asked, pointing at the candles.

"At your service."

The dining table, with its lace cloth covering a length of deep blue material, held her blue-patterned antique china. A folded newspaper lay beside Jackson's plate at the head of the table. The sideboard held covered serving dishes, although they were empty. "Sounds like they're gathering," Liz whispered.

Jackson and Naomi took their seats at the table while Bert, the butler, stood at attention with his back to the wall. Liz used her phone to snap a photo, then backed out, pulling the door shut behind her.

Out in the rotunda, five of the guests had gathered. Coming around the last curve of the staircase was Paul, puffing even while descending the stairs. His Sherlock costume fit better than his teammate's Watson outfit. Cherise lounged seductively against the banister, but she had obviously fudged on her size, ordering a size two when a six would have fit better. Spotting the mother and daughter team, Liz pressed her lips together hard to keep from laughing. Their costumes fit, but Louise wore her shawl over the Watson costume, while Penny wore her Sherlock deerstalker hat sideways, with what should have been the front and back brims sticking out over her ears.

Penny whispered in Liz's ear. "I still haven't found the contents of Mother's makeup case, but she doesn't seem to be worried."

"But her medicine?"

"I called her doctor. He phoned in a replacement prescription. I can pick it up tomorrow."

Liz nodded, wondering if she'd be presented with a bill from the pharmacy. She'd be glad to pay it. At least, for the evening, things were calmer.

Vivian stepped forward, her arm tucked through Jeremy's. Jeremy shook her off. "Watson, get hold of yourself," he said.

Vivian giggled. "Sorry." She pulled a pen and her Sherlock pad of paper from her pocket. "Bring on the clues."

Reminding herself that she was a Victorian lady, Liz nodded graciously, feeling her cameo earrings dance. "The actors are ready and waiting." She handed out folded programs, grateful that she'd made them herself so she had been able to update them with the last-minute casting change.

Character Portrayed:	Actor
James Braithwaite	*Jackson Cross*
Nettie Braithwaite	*Naomi Mason*
Dr. Philip Fitzhugh	*David Mills*
Godfrey Denshaw, newspaper publisher	*Rob Carver*
Constable Liddle	*George Hughes*
Doyle, the butler	*Bert Worth*

"Not every actor will be in every scene," Liz explained. "Tonight's Act One takes place one evening in the dining room of James and Nettie Braithwaite. Their butler, Doyle, will wait at table." She opened the door. "Follow me."

Liz led the way into the dining room, where the actors sat like mannequins in the candlelight. Keeping her voice low, Liz lined up the guests along the wall to watch Act One. Mary Ann and Sadie eased in behind them. Liz introduced Mr. and Mrs. Braithwaite and Doyle.

"Remember to watch carefully. Anything, even the most innocent remark, can be a clue." Liz turned and nodded for Act One to begin.

James Braithwaite, in a heavy British accent, read aloud two short snippets from the evening newspaper. One was an "advert for a bagatelle board game" and another article revealed a new method for the layman to determine the sex of fertilized chicken eggs by wrinkles on the shells. Nettie Braithwaite drank her tea, shaking her head over the board game and rolling her eyes about the egg discovery. Doyle stepped forward once, took the teapot from the sideboard, and refilled her cup. Then he retired to the wall and once again stared straight ahead, as if he were just part of the dining room furniture.

Liz grinned. She could feel the magic as they were transported to another continent in a past century. She glanced quickly at her Holmes/Watson pairs. Jeremy was watching the scene as if he had a movie camera operating behind his eyes. Vivian was studying Jeremy as much as the actors, her disappointment obvious that his eyes never veered toward her.

Penny's gaze wandered around the room, but Louise leaned forward, her eyes fixed on the unfolding scene. With her stick-thin arms, she reminded Liz of a starving bird waiting for a worm to emerge from its hole in the ground.

The slight curl of Cherise's glossy lips revealed her opinion of the amateur acting. Beside her, leaning against the wall, Paul's eyelids drooped over his brown eyes so that they almost hid the intelligence that gleamed there.

JAMES *(turning to an inside page of the newspaper):* *I say, listen to this!*

NETTIE *(nibbling a scone with jam):* Yes, James?

JAMES: *You remember the Dickens rare edition I bought last week?*

NETTIE *(yawning):* How could I not? You've talked of nothing else to anyone who stops by.

JAMES *(sounding slightly annoyed):* It's a privilege to share such a treasure with the world. It would be selfish for me to keep it to myself.

NETTIE *(raising one eyebrow):* Yes, dear. What did you want me to listen to?

JAMES: *After Godfrey saw my book, he wrote an article about it. Listen. (He pompously reads the article aloud. Then his smile fades, and he slaps the newspaper on the table.) Godfrey should have placed this article on the front page. He's my friend, for heaven's sake! This is important news to many collectors*

NETTIE: *He's doing you a service, my dear. You keep*

saying that your rare edition is valuable. Thieves on the street could read about it on the stands if dear Godfrey had made it front page news.

JAMES (frowning): You could be right.

(Doyle steps forward and pours more tea for James, but Nettie delicately refuses a refill.)

NETTIE: Shouldn't you keep the book under lock and key instead of displaying it so prominently in the drawing room?

JAMES (standing): What good is having the rare edition if I can't have it out to read? (Leaves the room.)

NETTIE (mumbling): Read? More like show off. (She exits, followed by Doyle.)

Liz stepped in front of her guests. "This is the end of Act One. You are allowed to remain in the room to look around and take notes or photos, but only for five minutes." She glanced at her watch. "Starting now."

She moved into the butler's place against the wall and waited. Mary Ann gave her a thumbs-up as she and Sadie stole out of the room. There was very little whispering among the guests, but individuals scribbled notes, careful to hide them from rival teams. How odd, though, to see three Sherlock Holmeses and three John Watsons milling around her dining room. Liz glanced out into the rotunda where the actors chatted. Jackson and Naomi had been fantastic and hadn't misspoken a single line of dialogue.

At the end of five minutes, Liz announced, "Act One is officially closed. Feel free to use any room downstairs except this one to privately discuss your ideas as a team. Remember, no clue is too insignificant to write down to solve the crime that is coming."

Liz smiled as Penny and her mother left. Louise had discarded her shawl and was whispering animatedly in her daughter's ear.

Cherise's words to Paul were loud enough for all to hear. "With my acting experience, it's second nature for me to read between the lines. That's all it takes to solve a mystery." Paul grunted a response and tried to edge his bulk around her.

Jeremy and Vivian smiled like Cheshire cats as they left. Viv appeared delighted with the instructions to go off somewhere privately to discuss their clues. Relieved that Act One had gone off without a hitch, Liz leaned over the table, cupped her hand behind a candle, and blew softly. It was then that Jeremy's voice carried from the rotunda. "I agree. Totally hokey performance."

Liz froze over the candelabra, her spirits sinking. *What a start to the mystery weekend.* A sick actor, the missing money, the missing jewelry and medication, and now the guests' judgment that the acting was "hokey." Then she stood up straight. What did Jeremy know about it? That was only one opinion. Liz thought her friends had been terrific.

If only the missing wages, jewelry, and medicine were just a matter of opinion.

On Saturday morning Liz ignored her apprehension as she placed a Victorian breakfast on the sideboard and lit the candles under the chafing dishes. Flames leaped in the corner fireplace, but she'd removed the candelabra and fancy lace overlay from the table.

With the bright overhead electric lights and the weak November light at the windows, it barely resembled the room from Act One.

She was carrying in the pitcher of orange juice when her guests arrived, in twos and singly, for their London breakfast. "After you take your seats," Liz said, "I'll explain what I'm serving this morning and why it's authentic Victorian London food. Some foods this weekend will appear foreign to you. Other dishes may be familiar if you've traveled to England, as some dishes from Victorian times are still popular today."

"Is this the same dining room?" Louise whispered to her daughter. She pulled her shawl more closely around her shoulders. "It doesn't smell like breakfast."

Liz smiled. "I can tell you why. Much of what was eaten for breakfast during Victorian times was created with leftovers from dinner the night before. Without refrigeration, leftover cooked meats and vegetables needed to be eaten before they spoiled." At Louise's frown, she added, "I made these dishes myself, however, and you can rest assured that everything was refrigerated overnight before I cooked it up this morning."

"Well it smells good," Vivian said. "I like that I'm eating what Sherlock Holmes might have eaten. My book club members would love this idea. It puts me in the right mood for Act Two this morning."

Liz lifted the lid on the first casserole pan, added a serving spoon, and started around the table. "This first dish has the charming name of 'bubble and squeak.' Mr. Braithwaite from Act One loves it, and I hope you will too. I've cooked it in individual patties, but it can also be fried in a pie-shaped dish, then cut into wedges." She paused between the mother and daughter, waiting while they helped themselves. "It was a practical way to use up leftover meat and mashed potatoes—or mash, as Londoners say—plus sprouts and cabbage."

She moved and waited while Viv and Jeremy each took a patty.

"Where's the name come from?" Penny asked, taking a tentative bite.

"It has to do with the cooking," Liz explained. "It makes bubbles when it's frying, and when you turn the patties over, bits of potato catch in the pan and make a squeaking sound.

"These are meat rissoles," she said, uncovering the next container. "Different kinds are made around the world, but this is the type eaten in Great Britain." Again, she circled the table. "They are made from minced meat, usually beef or lamb, mixed with bread crumbs and onion, without the pastry covering that you find in other countries. As you see, they resemble irregular meatballs. Rissoles are cooked in a frying pan. They can be eaten hot as part of a meal, like this morning, or cold as a snack with tomato sauce or relish, or sliced in a sandwich."

Paul tucked a napkin into his shirt collar. "It may have a different name than bubble and squeak, but it sounds like just another way to use leftovers. Is that what we're eating here? Your leftovers?"

"Of course not." Mildly annoyed at the thinly veiled attack, Liz tried to reassure them. "I cooked the beef and lamb yesterday specifically for this morning's breakfast."

Cherise dabbed her lips with her napkin and pushed her plate away. She had not touched either food. "I was excited about having special London breakfasts, but I expected jam tarts and puff pastries, not refried roast beef and mashed-up vegetables."

Penny nodded like a bobble head in agreement. "Mother can't handle all this greasy fried food. She likes flaky croissants for breakfast."

Liz forced herself to keep smiling. "I did press the patties and meatballs between layers of paper towels to absorb any excess fat." *And the average croissant has several pats of butter hidden in its flaky layers.* "As I explained in the information I mailed out, I wanted to give you a well-rounded Sherlock experience by taking you back to Victorian London at every opportunity."

Jeremy cleared his throat and waited until all eyes were on him. "I did some research on Sherlock Holmes before I came. When he wasn't detecting, he appreciated a good breakfast." He raised his voice. "The housekeeper at 221B Baker Street, Mrs. Hudson, provided Holmes with hearty breakfasts such as kidneys, kedgeree, ham and eggs, and even chicken curry."

"That's very interesting. Thank you." Liz nodded. "I could have fixed ham and eggs, I suppose, but it didn't sound very British, and the others didn't sound like breakfast food. And what is kedgeree?"

"A dish still enjoyed in Britain today. Kedgeree is made from boiled rice, chopped hard-boiled egg, and cold fish, all fried together in one pan with spices."

Another British breakfast recipe for using up the leftovers. Most of her guests dug into their food, apparently willing to try it now that they had been assured of its authenticity, and the talk turned to their favorite Sherlock Holmes books and film stars. Only Cherise still appeared disgruntled. Liz guessed she'd sneak in a trip next door to Naomi's Sweet Everything bakery later.

While the guests continued to talk, Liz inched out of the room and took the stairs two at a time up to the second floor. She met Sarah coming out of the room occupied that weekend by Vivian. "How are you coming with making up the beds?" she asked.

"I've done the Heirloom and the Amish rooms so far."

"Could you start cleaning up in the kitchen now instead? I'll finish the bed making."

"All right." Never one to ask for explanations, Sarah turned over the master key and headed downstairs, her footsteps barely discernible on the staircase.

With her heart racing, Liz went quickly through all four rooms on the second floor. She made the last two beds, wincing at the condition of Paul's and Cherise's rooms. If they were in that much disarray already, what condition would their rooms be in by the end of the weekend?

She didn't have time to worry about that now. Without rummaging through personal items, Liz scanned all visible surfaces in the bedrooms and adjoining baths, looking for signs of the missing jewelry and blood pressure medication. Quick peeks under beds and dressers produced nothing either.

Pausing at the top of the stairs, Liz strained to listen for movement below. Sounds from the kitchen told her the guests were still in the dining room. Heading up to the third floor, she quickly made up the Sunrise and Sunset Rooms, and freshened the shared bathroom. Both bedrooms were neat, both beds already made. There was no visible jewelry or medication.

After locking Penny's room, Liz descended the staircase and was in the library when she heard the first guests head upstairs after breakfast.

An hour later, after setting up the library as a London police station, Liz attached the placard announcing *Act Two* to the closed library door, which she locked to keep the guests out.

Liz headed for the kitchen, then stopped short in the doorway at the sight of Paul Levine down on all fours with his head in her lower cupboard. Liz waited, not moving, not breathing. She watched him go from the cupboard to her pantry. Was he snooping, or was he hungry?

He stood and opened her freezer, then turned, startled to discover he was being watched.

"May I help you?" Liz asked, trying to keep the suspicion out of her voice.

"Just wanting something to eat." He hiked up his pants, looking sheepish. "Your London food was all right, but it wasn't very filling."

"I'm sorry to hear that," Liz said, although she knew for a fact that he had consumed two servings of each dish, plus Cherise's untouched food, and that was just while she'd been in the room. "There are two different London dishes on the breakfast menu for tomorrow. I'll remember to fix extra. Are you looking for something specific?"

"Just a snack." He leaned back against the counter. "I couldn't find anything."

Liz pointed to the bowl of fresh fruit and basket of energy bars on the counter behind him.

He laughed. "Too healthy for me," he said, squeezing around her. Liz turned sideways to let him through the kitchen door.

Hairs prickled on the back of her neck as she watched Paul climb the stairs. Liz didn't believe he'd been in her kitchen to find food. Had she interrupted a theft in progress? Could he have been the one who'd taken the wage envelope from the desk? If so, how could she ever prove it? Thinking back, she didn't know exactly what time she'd last seen the bank envelope. And what about Louise's jewelry and medicine? Had Paul taken it? She'd seen no sign of it in her room. Maybe he'd forgotten his own blood pressure medication? But if so, why not just go to the pharmacy for some more?

Her gut reaction registered certainty on one thing though. He'd been searching for something, and it hadn't been a snack. She'd be sure to keep an eye on him for the rest of the weekend.

5

Dressed in her long skirt and lacy blouse, Liz met her guests in the rotunda at ten thirty. She waited till they'd all gathered in front of the library door, resplendent in their Sherlock Holmes and John Watson garb. Penny even had her hat on correctly. It was an impressive sight, except for Paul, who looked as if he'd slept in his costume.

Liz peeked around the doorway into the Sew Welcome Shop to let her friends know the next performance would be soon. But both Sadie and Mary Ann were busy with customers.

"Act Two?" Liz mouthed to Mary Ann, pointing to her watch.

"We'll try," Mary Ann mouthed back.

Liz nodded, hoping things slowed down long enough for one or both of them to pop over and watch the next act.

"I hope you have your pads and pens for noting more clues." Liz pointed to her sign. "Act Two takes place in a local London police station. In this scene, Constable Liddle is taking a report from an agitated James Braithwaite."

She opened the library door and motioned for them to stay near the door for the best view. Liz couldn't help grinning. George Hughes, a Pleasant Creek police officer, really looked the part of the constable. With his thinning hair and a paunch, he wore his British police costume as if it had been made for him personally.

Liz ran a critical eye over the room. Had she missed anything? She'd mocked up a counter for George to stand behind. A sign on the wall read *Peterborough Street Station* and was flanked by two wanted posters, which added to the atmosphere. She'd moved the couch away from the wall and set up a canvas cot behind it for a prison cell. She thought with satisfaction that she'd created a reasonable likeness of a Victorian police station.

CONSTABLE LIDDLE (pencil poised): Did I hear you right? (Clears throat.) You want to report a missing . . . book?

JAMES BRAITHWAITE (frustrated): Not just any book, Liddle! It's a rare edition by Charles Dickens. You do know who that is, don't you?

CONSTABLE (offended): I guess I know about The Pickwick Papers as much as anyone else.

JAMES: Well this is a much more valuable first edition. It's his Sketches by Boz, published in 1836. The book was in perfect condition.

CONTABLE (writing): Anything else to identify it? Did you write your name inside?

JAMES (gasping): Write in it? Are you mad? (He shakes his head.) But it contains sixteen colored plates illustrated by George Cruikshank. That should be enough to identify it.

CONSTABLE (muttering under his breath as he makes notes): All right. We'll contact you if it turns up.

JAMES: I'm not done. I'm offering a reward of a hundred pounds for the return of my book. Whom should

I notify to get the word out? A reporter?

CONSTABLE: No need. The reporters on this beat will be notified when they show up this morning. You can bet your theft and reward will make the front page of the morning Globe.

JAMES: But why aren't the reporters already here? The longer it takes before anyone reads about my reward, the less chance I have to get it back. Get on the case, Liddle! (He pounds his fist on the counter.)

CONSTABLE: Sir, I have a murder, two beatings, and a bank robbery to work on. Your missing Dickens book, well, we'll get to it when we get to it.

JAMES (raising voice): Where's your superintendent? I demand to speak to him! I— (He clutches his shirt front, groans, and staggers backward.)

CONSTABLE (hurrying to the front of the counter): Here, sir, lie down. (He helps James to the empty cot in prisoner's cell.) I'll send for the doctor right away.

When the actors froze in place, Liz stepped forward. "This is the end of Act Two. As before, you may remain in the room, look around, and take notes or photos, but only for five minutes." She glanced at her watch. "Starting now."

The guests surged forward. Vivian studied the notes taken by the constable. Penny scribbled her own notes. Fingering his good luck gold piece, Jeremy scanned the scene as if memorizing it. He and Vivian went to sit on the front porch in the weak November sunshine, cold as it was, presumably to have more privacy. Cherise dragged a shuffling Paul toward the dining room to talk, her bubbly chatter echoing in the rotunda. Penny and Louise slowly climbed the staircase to their rooms. Liz heaved a sigh of relief about Louise. The pharmacy had called, saying the prescription was ready, so a medical crisis had been averted.

But what about her jewelry? As soon as she had a minute to herself, Liz needed to do some more digging.

Liz turned back to the frozen tableau. "You can move now," she said, grinning as Jackson sat up on the cot and George unsnapped the chin strap on his helmet. "Well done, guys."

Jackson straightened his cravat, which had gone askew when he collapsed. "Was it overly dramatic, do you think?"

"You mean melodramatic?" Liz shook her head decisively. "Not at all. The guests were riveted. They took notes at the end while you were lying there. They all observed this scene very seriously." Liz glanced out into the rotunda and lowered her voice. "I expect they think that the theft of the book is the crime they have to solve. They're in for a surprise tomorrow."

George tucked his hat under his arm and picked up his truncheon. "That was fun. I'm kind of sorry now that it's the only scene I'm in." He glanced at his watch. "Gotta run. I need to get home and change for my shift. Should I drop off my costume at the playhouse?"

"That'd be great, George," Liz said. "And again, thank you so much for agreeing to do this."

"No problem." With a wave, he headed to the foyer and on outside.

Liz rolled the table she'd used for the counter out of the room. Jackson had folded the cot and stashed it in its drawstring bag. In just a few minutes, they had taken down the signs and posters and pushed the furniture back into place. As Liz bent to straighten the crumpled area rug, she felt a mild throb in her temple. She put her hand to her head.

"You all right?" Jackson asked. "Dizzy?"

"No, just a little headache. Probably from hunger. I served my first London breakfast this morning, but I don't remember eating anything myself."

"You can't run on fumes," Jackson scolded her. "By the way, how did they like your—er, what was it called?"

"This morning I served meat rissoles—those meatballs you liked—and the bubble and squeak. Neither one was a hit, even after I gave my little history of the recipes."

Jackson's eyes gleamed. "So you've got more?" At her nod, he grinned "Their loss is my gain."

"Are you inviting yourself to lunch?" Liz teased as they made their way to the kitchen. She pulled dishes from the refrigerator. "I'll warm them up, then go change back to the present century."

"Let me do it while you go change."

"Thanks, Jackson. Be right back."

Liz gulped down two aspirin after changing out of her Victorian skirt and blouse, then rejoined him. He'd already reheated the remaining meat rissoles and found some barbecue sauce, and she joined him at the table with a turkey sandwich of her own.

"You sure your head's all right?" Jackson asked between bites.

"It will be." Liz leaned back in her chair. "That isn't really what's bothering me." She filled him in on the missing items, then finished with finding one of her guests snooping around in her kitchen cupboards. "Something odd is going on."

Jackson laid down his fork. "Can I help? Or are you going to call the police?"

"Penny declined my offer to call them, so maybe the jewelry isn't valuable."

Jackson folded his arms. "Or maybe she suspects her mother mislaid it and can't remember where she put it."

"That's possible. Her mother does seem to be rather confused." She took another bite. "I hope their things will show up, and I'll probably find the wages envelope where I laid it down." She grinned. "I've had a few senior moments of my own lately."

By the time they finished eating and Jackson left to put in a couple hours at his furniture store, her headache was mostly gone. She grinned to herself, speculating on which remedy had been the magical cure: the aspirin and food, or Jackson's undivided attention in her cozy kitchen.

As she loaded the dishwasher, she wondered which restaurants her guests had chosen for lunch, then admitted to herself that she didn't much care. She just appreciated the peace and quiet for a couple hours. She still hoped to catch a quick nap.

But first, the decorating. She grabbed her box full of props borrowed from the playhouse. The sitting room would be fairly easy to transform into James and Nettie Braithwaite's bedroom. It already had the original tall windows, with sheer curtains pulled back. The carved antique sofas could stay, but she scooped the current issues of *Town & Country* off the coffee table, replacing them with a gold music box and a painted vase filled with silk lilacs. An empty perfume bottle, a glass oil lamp, and some shaving gear changed the walnut desk into a bureau. Liz opened the recliner and put the footrest up, then converted it into a bed with quilts and pillows. She planned to light a fire in the fireplace before three o'clock. Gazing around the room, she decided to turn off the crystal chandelier and use only the wall sconces for light.

She was attaching the *Act Three* sign to the sitting room door when the front door opened and two people entered. One was an Amish woman, who nodded at Liz as she headed for the Sew Welcome Shop. Close behind her was David Mills.

"Hi, David." Liz glanced at her watch. "I don't need you until three."

"I know, but I thought I'd practice a little more. I want to sound more natural as the doctor."

"I'm sure you'll do fine. Say, have you done your magic show for the kids yet?"

"Yes, this morning." He smiled so that his eyes crinkled, giving his sharply angled face a softer look. "You should have seen them. Some of those poor kids have life-threatening diseases, but they're so brave. So are their parents. Seeing them forget their pain and laugh at my magic tricks—well, it's hard to explain."

"It lightens their heavy load, at least for a while, and that's wonderful," Liz said. "I'm afraid that acting in a couple of skits here won't be as life changing, but I think the guests are having fun."

He pointed to the closed sitting room door. "Do you mind if I hang out in there for an hour or so and run through my lines?"

"No, not at all. Just keep the door closed so no one crossing the rotunda can look in. I think all the guests are out right now, having lunch or sightseeing."

"Will do."

Back in her private quarters, Liz stashed the box of items she'd removed from the sitting room and glanced longingly at her bed—a short nap would be lovely—but knew she needed to do one more thing before napping. In the kitchen, she got out some wicker baskets and divided serving trays to fill with snacks for the guests to enjoy after Act Three. She'd provide her usual coffee hour fare of delicious baked goods, plus a few extra treats, and they could study their clues. She piled the island with food, then sat down on one of the stools. On the serving trays she arranged cheese and crackers and mini banana nut muffins from the bakery, then covered everything with plastic wrap. Just before serving she'd add some sliced fruit. On a normal weekend at the inn, when the guests came and went and had no fixed schedule for anything, she provided coffee and cookies in the sitting room. But this weekend, Liz felt she should do more since the guests stayed on the premises so much of the time.

She carried everything to the sideboard in the dining room. Then she returned to the kitchen, wiped the counters and appliances, refilled Beans's water bowl, and straightened the desk where notes and recipes and lists seemed to multiply like rabbits.

Liz eyed the bowl of fresh fruit on the counter. She was a bit hungry. A crisp Jonathan apple would make a healthier snack than the last piece of leftover cheesecake in the fridge. *The apple it is.* She grabbed a plate and reached for her favorite paring knife from the wood block on the counter. Only it wasn't there. She looked in the dishwasher, but it wasn't in the silverware basket either. Now she was puzzled. It wasn't in the sink, and she hadn't left it in the fridge on a plate or anywhere else she could think of. So where was it?

Aggravated with herself for misplacing it, she tried to remember what she'd done with it. "This is silly." She had half a dozen paring knives. She found another, then cored and sliced her apple. When Jeremy, Vivian, and Cherise trailed in, she asked them if they'd borrowed her paring knife and had taken it to their room for some reason. "It's fine if you did. I just need it back." No one admitted to using it though.

Liz knew she was overreacting, but having the knife disappear just added to her anxiety about the other missing things at the inn. First the wages, then Louise's jewelry and medication, and now her knife. This had to be more than David practicing his pickpocketing skills. Had Paul taken it when he was snooping around her kitchen? But if so, why?

Something else was going on at the inn that weekend, something mysterious and unplanned. Liz shook her head. *And I'm no Sherlock Holmes.*

6

Liz was reconsidering her menu for the next morning's breakfast when Beans wandered into the kitchen. His stumpy tail gave a half-hearted wag as he headed for his kibble. He crunched several pieces, then went to stand in front of the refrigerator where hot air blew from the vent at the bottom.

"Getting your feet warm?" Liz asked.

Beans gave her a look as if waiting for something.

"If you're hoping for a piece of bologna, you snatched it all earlier."

He stared at Liz, unblinking, and let out a low *woof.*

She reached down and scratched behind one of his ears. "All right, but don't tell Jackson I gave you some of his food."

As she fed Beans bits of rissole, Liz considered the complaints about her fare that morning. Should she reconsider her menu and fix additional food for Sunday morning? No, she could pop next door to Sweet Everything if she decided she needed to offer more.

She hadn't realized how much extra work the mystery weekend would entail. Next time she'd charge more. If there *was* a next time, and the jury was still out on that.

Liz closed her eyes, weary from thinking, and took a few deep breaths. Now would be a good time to sneak off for a twenty-minute rest in her darkened bedroom.

"I need to talk to you."

Liz nearly jumped out of her skin at the whisper in her ear. She whirled around so fast she nearly fell off the kitchen stool. "Jeremy. You startled me." She hadn't heard him come in. "What can I do for you?"

Wearing jeans and a sweater, he craned his neck toward the door and looked sheepish. Liz tensed. Who was he hiding from? Vivian, his partner in solving crime? She braced herself to deal with a complaint that the woman had attached herself to him too much or too often. She'd been trailing in his shadow ever since he arrived.

"Can I help you?" she prodded.

"I know you said we might get pickpocketed this weekend, but I wanted to be sure we would get our things back."

"You certainly will." Liz smiled to look reassuring, even though only a handkerchief had been turned in to her for safekeeping. "Is it something you want back right away, or can I keep it until the end of the weekend? What was taken?"

He laughed, shuffled his feet, and pink spread from his neck to the tips of his ears. "I'm not even sure when it happened," he said, "but I guess that's the sign of a good pickpocket, right?" Liz nodded, but remained silent. "Um, you know how every writer has good luck charms?"

Liz didn't know that, but she nodded anyway. "Your gold coin?"

He laughed, but it sounded forced. "No. My rabbit's foot. It was in my pocket," he explained. "I'm stunned that I didn't notice when it happened."

"Well, I'll return it Sunday before you leave, unless you need it before then." If the rumors were true that he hadn't sold a new book in years, she suspected he needed a more potent charm than that anyway. He was clearly reluctant to leave the rabbit's foot with her till then. She hoped he didn't ask for it back since it hadn't been turned in yet. She didn't want Jeremy seeing her get it back from David, or David's secret pickpocketing days would be over already. Beans plopped down by the refrigerator again and gave Jeremy a woebegone expression, as if Jeremy had his full sympathy.

The mystery writer forced a hearty laugh and patted Beans. "Well, since you don't have a black cat on the premises," he said, "I guess I'll be fine till tomorrow without it." He left.

"Okay." Liz reached down to scratch Beans behind the ears and whispered, "I've always wondered why a rabbit's foot is good luck. It didn't do the rabbit much good, did it?"

Maybe it was time to talk to David. She needed to remind him to turn things in so she could put them in the safe. She hoped he was still rehearsing in the sitting room. But when could the pickpocketing have happened? When had David been around Jeremy? It would have taken only a moment. They would just need to pass each other anywhere in the inn. David had seemed really nervous about performing this afternoon. Maybe knowing how successful he'd been with the rabbit's foot would give him a boost of confidence.

But as she headed toward the sitting room, Liz spotted him near the door of Sew Welcome. She started to call out, but something stopped her. He looked odd there. Tense. Watchful. Liz pulled back into the kitchen doorway and waited, but he didn't go into the shop. Instead, he peeked around the corner into the shop, then jerked back out of sight.

She waited. Suddenly he crossed the rotunda halfway and ducked beneath the staircase, out of sight. *Curiouser and curiouser.*

Moving back further, Liz peered around the kitchen doorway. A plump Amish woman, probably in her fifties, emerged from the fabric store holding a cloth shopping bag. Liz recognized the woman. Rhoda Miller often bought material at the Sew Welcome Shop to make her traditional faceless Amish dolls. Recently widowed, Rhoda sold the dolls from a little store at her farm home and also at the local craft markets throughout the year. Even though Liz's own mother's Amish name had been Miller, Liz was no relation to this woman.

As Liz waited, Rhoda tightened the strings of her bonnet, then headed out to the foyer and on outside. David peered around the staircase, then followed the woman. He hesitated a moment in the foyer, then slipped outside. Liz started after him—she needed to ask him about the rabbit's foot—but his secretive behavior made her think twice.

Instead, she went into the sitting room where the windows overlooked the street. Standing behind the sheer curtain, Liz watched. David kept a discreet distance, but he continued down the sidewalk after Rhoda. Liz leaned closer to the window to see down the street. Only when Rhoda met a younger Amish woman and crossed the street with her did David veer off in another direction.

Why in the world was David following the Amish woman? And he *was* following her, no matter how nonchalant he tried to appear. Why stalk her? She was old enough to be his mother.

Had David overheard Rhoda say something in Sew Welcome that was so unusual it made him want to follow her? Liz watched until they were both out of sight, then dropped the curtain back in place. Had the Amish woman told Sadie or Mary Ann that she felt sick? Or maybe she was afraid of something? Had David followed her to her buggy to make sure she was all right out of the goodness of his heart?

Deep in thought, Liz headed toward the sewing shop. Maybe Mary Ann and Sadie could shed some light on David's odd behavior.

When she stepped across the threshold, Mary Ann glanced up from where she was seated behind the counter where they cut the yard goods. She blinked and ducked below the counter for a moment, then popped back up. Beside her, Sadie grinned at Liz like a cat caught in the cream.

Liz regarded her two friends. "Did I interrupt something?"

"Not a thing," Mary Ann said.

Sadie rolled her eyes. "Just arguing."

"We were not." Mary Ann rolled her eyes. "Sadie and I can't agree on how to decorate the shop for Thanksgiving. She wants to make turkey decorations out of balls of colored yarn with drinking straws stuck in them. And she wants to put pink jackets on them! *Pink!* Did you ever?"

"Don't forget the inflatable turkey leg decorations I found online."

Mary Ann sighed. "Who could forget?"

Liz couldn't quite picture such a thing. "Mary Ann, what do *you* want to decorate with?"

"Something more traditional, since we're in Amish country. I was thinking along the lines of autumn-colored fabric bunting. It's actually made for front porches, but it could be hung inside too, over doorways or under windows or along the front edge of the counters."

Liz nodded understanding.

"And," Mary Ann added, "I thought a more natural kind of decor this year. I found wreaths made from live plants like olive and eucalyptus, magnolia, even pussy willow."

Liz sighed. "And wouldn't the eucalyptus smell wonderful?"

"Only if you like it." Sadie sniffed. "I think it stinks."

Mary Ann ignored her. "I was thinking of having a craft table where women—and even older children—could make a Thanksgiving decoration to take home. I found a craft idea for making chenille pumpkins."

Liz gave her a quizzical look. "Chenille, like bedspreads?"

"Yes and no. The fluffy material is made into chenille straws, like fuzzy pipe cleaners. Orange for pumpkins, green for stems, red for apples, whatever. You use wooden spools, the kind that thread used to come on, to hold them together. They're really cute."

Sadie sniffed. "Inflatable turkey leg decorations are more original."

Mary Ann ignored her so automatically that Liz wondered if that was the secret to their long-standing friendship. "One other thing," Mary Ann said. "I found a guest book that would be fun to have customers sign during Thanksgiving. They give their name and list one thing that inspires their gratitude."

"I like that too," Liz said, wondering how to turn the conversation to what she really wanted to talk about. "But I also like Sadie's quirkier ideas. I think they capture her personality, and the customers will think it's endearing. By the way, quiet morning?"

"Slow as molasses in January." Sadie waved an arm around the empty shop. "Or molasses in November."

"Say, I noticed Rhoda Miller leaving earlier," Liz said, trying to sound casual. "Was she getting more material for her faceless dolls?"

Sadie nodded. "She does good business all year round now, with craft fairs and mail order."

"Lots of tourists collect them," Mary Ann said. "Rhoda sells every one of them that she makes: *Mutter* dolls, *Kinder* dolls, *Bubbies*, old bearded *Grossvater* dolls, and plump *Grossmutter* dolls—entire families. She even makes tiny Amish quilts for doll-size beds. They're beautiful."

Liz leaned against the counter and folded her arms. "I couldn't help noticing that when Rhoda left, she looked preoccupied, even worried. I hope she's all right."

"She's always serious," Mary Ann said. "Polite, for sure, and not given to hijinks like our Sadie here."

"And more's the pity," Sadie retorted. "I know how to have fun."

"So Rhoda was fine then? And her family?"

Mary Ann shrugged. "They're fine as far as I know. Why?"

Liz opened her mouth to ask if they'd noticed David following Rhoda out of the inn, but before she could, Mary Ann's phone rang.

"Heath? How good to hear your voice!" Mary Anne's face lit up. "How are you? And Charlotte? And the boys?" She nodded as she

listened, but then her smile faded. "Oh, I'm sorry to hear that . . .
Of course you can bring the boys by. I'd love to have them. No, don't
cancel your plans. I'd be thrilled to keep them overnight . . . Sounds
good. I'll expect you in an hour."

"What happened?" Sadie asked the minute she hung up.

"It's my son's wedding anniversary tomorrow, and he was taking
Charlotte overnight to a place that is special to them. A friend was
going to watch their three boys overnight, but the sitter has stomach
flu now."

"Grossmutter to the rescue then?" Liz asked.

"Yes, and I couldn't be happier. Sadie, I hate to ask, but—"

"Sure. Run along. I can watch the store for the last couple of hours."

"And tomorrow until they pick up the boys? I'm not sure when
it will be. We don't have to open up tomorrow for special hours." She
turned to Liz. "We wanted to see your mystery unfold."

"Never fear, Sadie's here." Sadie's eyes twinkled roguishly. "I'll fill
you in on what happens. Maybe I'll even redecorate while you're gone."

Alarm briefly crossed Mary Ann's face, then she laughed. "I'd
better get home and get ready for company. Three boys should keep
me plenty busy."

"Have fun with your grandsons," Liz said. "I'd better get back to
work myself." Her stomach growled and she grinned sheepishly. "I've
been hungry all day." Sadie sometimes kept a wooden bowl of miniature
candy bars under the counter, out of sight of customers. "I'll just grab
one tiny bit of chocolate and get back to work."

She started around the counter to reach for the candy, but Mary
Ann blocked her way. Liz stopped, mystified. But then Mary Ann
reached below and set the wooden bowl on the counter. Liz took one,
but she recalled the feeling when she'd entered the shop—that Mary
Ann was hiding something.

First David, now Mary Ann.

With a wave, she left the shop. She still had no idea why David had followed Rhoda. And Liz couldn't ask him without admitting that she had been watching *him* watch *her.* No. It would remain another unanswered question.

For now, at least.

7

Glancing at her watch as she left Sew Welcome, Liz savored the last of her chocolate. There was just time for that short nap.

She pulled the curtains in her bedroom, kicked off her shoes, and crawled under her quilt. Lying perfectly still, eyes closed, she deliberately tensed and relaxed each muscle of her body. Sometimes that put her right to sleep.

But not this afternoon. Her body might be motionless, but her mind flitted in rapid succession from one thing to another: David's odd behavior following the Amish woman, the unpopularity of her London breakfast, missing items not accounted for by her pickpocket . . .

Liz finally quit trying to relax and got up. She stretched, combed her hair, and put a smile on her face. On the way to the dining room, she was met by Vivian.

"Liz, I need to report something." She laughed self-consciously.

"What is it?"

Her eyes flashed with an excitement as she peered over her half glasses. "My watch was pickpocketed!" She waved her bare wrist as if to prove it. "I mean, it has this stretchy band that sometimes pulls the little hairs on my arm, but when it was taken, I didn't feel a thing."

Liz grinned at her thrill at being a victim, as if she'd been a wallflower waiting to be picked and now it was finally her turn to dance. "I'm glad you're glad," Liz said, making a mental note to make sure David was the one pocketing things from the guests.

"I'm having so much fun this weekend!" Vivian practically danced in her black sparkly ballet flats. "Well, I just wanted to report it. I must get back to Jeremy." She tightened the corners of her mouth into a little smirk. "I think we have your little mystery solved."

"Already?" Liz asked in mock horror, knowing they couldn't have because the real crime hadn't been committed yet.

"Don't worry." Vivian laid her hand on Liz's arm. "We won't let on to the other teams." She ran fingers through her black hair. "It probably wasn't fair of us to team up in the first place."

"Oh?"

"You know, a mystery book club president and a mystery writer. We were bound to put two and two together faster than the others." She pressed a finger against her lips. "But I promise that mum's the word!" She turned and scurried back to the library.

Sarah joined Liz in the dining room and got busy cleaning up crumbs on the sideboard and tossing used napkins in the wastebasket.

Liz shook her head. "Why do we bother with a wastebasket in here? So few people seem to use it."

Sarah scraped at a piece of muffin ground into the carpet. "They have their minds on other things today, tracking down clues and such."

"I'm sorry for the extra work it's made for you," Liz said. "I'm glad we have a simpler schedule most weekends."

"I don't mind. In fact—"

An aggrieved voice called, "So that's where you got to!"

Liz took a deep breath, stood, and brushed off her knees. "Can I help you with something, Cherise?"

Cherise tossed her blonde mane and batted her false eyelashes. "Some of my jewelry was stolen!"

"Our pickpocket sure is busy," Liz said. "It's the third report I've had today." Cherise's mouth dropped open, and Liz stopped herself from grinning. That took some wind out of the starlet's sails, but not for long.

"I didn't know your pickpocket was allowed to take things from our rooms."

Please, Liz prayed, *not another theft like Louise suffered.* Liz kept a relaxed tone. "He doesn't go into anyone's room. Hopefully you've just mislaid your jewelry."

"I couldn't have. I left it in my room in my black velvet roll-up bag. Just now I went to put some on and it was gone."

"And you're absolutely sure you brought it? I've accidentally taken empty cases with me on trips sometimes, just grabbing my organizers and packing them, assuming something was in them. Is it possible you might have done that?"

Cherise frowned. "I'm ninety-nine percent positive that I packed it. But I guess I could look again."

"Thank you." Liz smiled, waiting for the starlet to leave, but she continued to block the dining room door. "Would you like a snack?" Liz finally asked.

Cherise ran her hands down the sides of her tight Dr. Watson coat. "I don't keep a figure like this by indulging."

"No, I don't suppose you do." Liz got the feeling that Cherise wanted her to say something else, but she had no idea what. "Well," Liz said, moving around her, "I have some things to do before our next mystery performance."

They crossed the rotunda together, but instead of climbing the staircase to her room, Cherise followed Liz into the kitchen. "You know, Liz, this would be a perfect time for me to see you in action. You know, the behind-the-scenes stuff of being an innkeeper. I really want to do my next role justice, so any insider tips on how I should talk or act, don't hesitate."

"All right. I'll give it some thought. I never thought of my job here as a role, although I suppose it is."

Cherise perched on a kitchen chair. "This innkeeper part could be my breakout role, the performance that catapults me into the big leagues."

The image of Cherise catapulting anywhere at all tempted Liz to laugh.

When it appeared that Cherise wouldn't budge without some "behind-the-scenes tips," Liz forced herself to focus on her question. "Let's see. When you run an inn, you need people skills to help strangers with different personalities enjoy eating together at breakfast. One thing I do that helps—"

"I know all about working with different personalities," Cherise said. "I mean, let me tell you." She tapped her manicured nails on the table. "My last movie—no, wait, the one before that—I had a director and makeup gal who simply *loathed* each other. Now I know you're wondering—why did they have anything to do with each other in the first place?"

Liz smiled, although that was the last thing she was wondering.

"Well, it was because she couldn't get my makeup right. First it made my face glow like a full moon under the stage lights. Then she fixed it, but the director said it gave me shadows under my eyes so bad I looked *forty*!"

Liz, who was forty, managed to keep a straight face as she carried Beans's water bowl to the sink to refill it. "So," Liz asked, "what was your secret? How did you manage to get your director and makeup artist working in harmony?"

"What?" Cherise blinked, looking puzzled. "They hated each other even worse by the time we finished shooting."

"One thing that helps people find common ground is—"

"Oh, nothing—and I mean *nothing*—would have worked with those two."

"Yes, that can happen sometimes." Liz fell back on a tried-and-true technique. "I'm sorry to interrupt our talk, but I need to make an important phone call." It was true. She needed to talk to David.

"Sure. No problem." When Liz didn't dial, Cherise waved a hand. "You go ahead. I'll wait."

"It's private, actually."

Cherise blinked a moment, and Liz waited for the implication to sink in. "Right. Okay." She stood. "I'll go upstairs and look again for my necklace."

"Good luck. Let me know if you find it."

Liz dialed David's number the minute Cherise's footsteps headed up the staircase. "Hi, David. I need to talk to you."

"I'm only a block away," he said. "I went home to get my costume for this afternoon. I'm coming back a few minutes early so I can practice one last time."

"Okay. I'm in the kitchen."

"I'll find you."

Five minutes later, David draped his costume bag over the back of a kitchen chair. "What's up?"

"I wondered if the pickpocketing was working, and if you had anything for me to lock in the safe."

"Yeah, I do." He dug deep into both pockets. From the right he pulled a rabbit's foot, and from the left he lifted a woman's watch. "This fuzzy thing belongs to the mystery writer. The watch belongs to the woman he's paired with." He grinned suddenly. "This was the easiest sleight of hand I ever did. Just strolled by them a couple times. She was so engrossed in keeping his attention and he was so occupied in avoiding her clutching hands that I doubt either of them even saw me."

"They didn't. They've both reported these things missing." Liz took both items. She hesitated then, but knew she had to ask. "Cherise also reported a necklace taken from her room."

"Like I said before, I don't go into anyone's room."

"That's what I figured." Liz bit her bottom lip. "Only—"

"If something really was taken from her room, one of the guests could be a genuine thief," David said. "Maybe he—or she—is taking advantage of the fact that people are expecting a pickpocket."

"I hadn't considered that, but I'm afraid you might be right. I should go help her look for the necklace, in case she simply misplaced it."

Upstairs Liz knocked on the door of the Rose of Sharon Room. When Cherise answered, Liz said, "I've come to help you look for your necklace if you haven't found it yet. Our pickpocket did 'lift' things from two people's pockets this morning, but he wasn't in your room."

Cherise stepped back and opened the door wide.

Liz stepped into the room and had to fight a strong urge to cry out. How could Cherise have trashed it like this since this morning?

The Rose of Sharon quilt lay in a pile on the floor, and the sheets were a rumpled wad. The French armoire was open, but a pile of wrinkled clothes lay on the floor beneath empty hangers. What bothered Liz the most, though, was the haphazard pile of antique books on the floor, books that Cherise had apparently scooped off the shelf to make room for her astounding array of makeup containers. The bed had been made up earlier, but no one would know it now.

"This is embarrassing," Cherise said.

Liz took a deep breath. Cherise was obviously used to having someone pick up after her. *You'd never make it as a real innkeeper.* Liz stooped to pick up the books by Indiana author Gene Stratton-Porter, making sure that *A Girl of the Limberlost* hadn't been torn. She stacked the novels in the corner out of the way.

"Don't be embarrassed by the condition of the room." Liz made every effort to sound gracious. "After all, it is yours for the weekend."

Frowning, Cherise glanced around the bedroom, clearly baffled. Shrugging, she pointed to her open suitcase on the bed. "That's why I'm embarrassed."

"I don't understand."

"Come look at this."

The silky silver lining of the suitcase had a tiny slit in the seam. Half hanging out of the seam was a ruby necklace. Liz leaned closer to examine it. Or was it was made from less valuable garnets? "It's beautiful," Liz said.

"I just found it when I felt a lump inside the lining."

"But how did it get there?"

"See the tiny slit cut there?"

"Are you saying your necklace was returned, but hidden there?"

"Go figure. Who would take my necklace just to return it? And why did they have to damage my luggage?"

Liz studied the slit in the lining. What had made the cut? Her missing knife? She glanced at Cherise out of the corner of her eye. Or could the movie starlet have done it herself? Was it a way to get the attention she was accustomed to? Liz had noticed her disappointment when no one asked for an autograph or fawned over her—except for Jeremy, when Vivian dropped her guard.

"I can't answer your questions," Liz admitted. "I'll remind everyone to lock their rooms when they leave. The Sew Welcome Shop is inside the inn, so the front door is open to the public during business hours. Even though we live in such a safe community, I imagine someone could come in and head up the staircase without being seen."

"You should get security cameras installed," Cherise said. "On the porch, in the rotunda, and on all the floors. That's what I have in my own house. You can't be too careful these days."

Liz took a deep breath. If it ever came to the point where that was required, her innkeeping days would be over. "As I said, we have a very safe community. And I do lock the front door at ten."

Cherise's mouth dropped open. "We can't go out after *ten*?" Her tone implied that she'd landed on Mars.

"I'm happy to lend a temporary house key to anyone who wants to stay out later. You just turn the key in afterward."

Cherise rolled that over in her mind. "How do you know that a previous guest didn't have a duplicate made before turning one in?"

"I don't for sure," Liz admitted, "but it's an original front door key. Duplicating an antique key would be more difficult."

"You could have a lot of extra copies of front door keys floating around out there."

Yes, I could. And the buck stops with me. Keep that in mind for your innkeeper role.

"I'm glad you got your necklace back, but do lock your door when you leave the room," Liz said.

Liz was downstairs when she heard Sadie's voice call from the shop.

"Liz, can you come here a minute?"

"Sure. What's up?"

A quirky smile tugged at Sadie's lips. "I want to show you something."

"Sure." Liz followed her inside the shop, hoping to keep it short. She dearly loved her friend, but at the moment she had little free time.

Sadie scooted around behind the cutting counter and rocked back and forth on the balls of her feet. Liz tilted her head. Something was up. That much was clear. But what?

"Mary Ann and I have a surprise for you," Sadie said. "I'm only sorry she isn't here to give it to you with me." She reached below the counter.

"Do I get my own bowl of candy?" Liz joked.

"Something better. At least, we hope you'll think so." Sadie laid a large flat box on the counter and practically bounced on her feet.

Liz lifted the lid and folded back white tissue paper.

Inside was a garment sewn from the most electric royal blue material Liz had ever seen. She lifted out a dress that appeared to be her size, made with a gored skirt, an hourglass shape, and sleeves that ballooned out.

Liz's mouth dropped open. "This is the dress I wanted to sew. You and Mary Ann made this yourselves? For me?"

Sadie beamed. "I spilled the coffee on your outfit on purpose. We needed the skirt and blouse to get an exact fit for the Victorian day dress. We wish we'd thought of it sooner, but at least you can wear it for the rest of the weekend."

"Words fail me." Liz moved around the counter and hugged Sadie tight.

"Hold it up in front of you so I can see how it will look."

Liz lifted the blue dress all the way out of the box. She blinked in surprise when she saw the trim at the hem.

"I thought it needed a little sprucing up," Sadie said, "so it didn't look so somber."

The "sprucing up" was a bright pink ribbon sewn around the entire bottom of the hem.

"It's just basted on, in case you don't like it."

Liz glanced up at the eagerness in Sadie's eyes. "I love it. And I can't wait to wear this stunning dress for Act Three." She gave her another hug. "I have to run now though."

"If there aren't any customers at three, I'll run over and watch the next act."

On the way across the rotunda, Liz noticed the door to the sitting room was ajar. She hoped no one had ignored her *Act Three* sign on the door and disturbed the bedroom setting she'd created. Stepping inside, she flipped on the chandelier to dispel the gloom of the overcast November afternoon. Nothing appeared out of place.

But when she turned off the overhead light to leave, she realized the ambient light would be too dim during the play. Running to the dining room, she grabbed the two candelabra and a box of matches from the sideboard. She added one candelabra to the mantel and one to the makeshift bureau. She made a mental note to come in just before the show and light the candles.

Back in the kitchen, she found a stray coffee cup one of the guests must have left for her on the counter. She took it to the sink and halted so abruptly that she dropped the cup, which shattered when it hit the sink's surface.

Her favorite knife—the one that had gone missing—was back.

Only it wasn't in the wood block knife holder now. It was stuck, up to the hilt, in a cantaloupe on the counter, as if the fruit had been stabbed to death.

Her heart pounded crazily, even though it was just fruit. No one was bleeding or hurt. Still, it felt like a threat—or a warning—to her.

What did it all mean? Had Cherise received a warning too when her necklace was taken and then returned? Maybe Cherise *hadn't* tried to get attention by faking a theft after all.

Liz examined the cantaloupe. There was nothing sinister about a knife inserted up to its handle, she told herself firmly, but why do it? Why not return it to the knife block?

What in the world was happening at her mystery weekend? Were the pranks just a big joke? Was someone sneaking in from outside to scare them? Or was one of her Sherlock fans really a madman—or woman—in disguise?

8

When Liz heard the front door open and close, followed by the laughing voices of Jeremy, Vivian, and, to Liz's surprise, Paul, she yanked the sticky knife out of the cantaloupe. The actors should arrive soon, and she had to be ready. Her own investigating would have to wait till later.

She gathered the sharp fragments of the shattered cup and placed them into the wastebasket. She walked to the kitchen door and glanced into the rotunda, waving at the trio of guests as they headed up the spiral staircase.

"Change and be back downstairs at three o'clock for Act Three," she called after them.

She had just finished stacking the dishes in the dishwasher when a woman's piercing scream echoed down the staircase into the rotunda. The sound bounced off the walls.

Liz sprinted to the stairs and took the steps two at a time. She craned her neck upward. Had the shout come from the second or third floor?

When she reached the second floor, both Cherise and Vivian were in the hall. "What was that?" Vivian asked.

"It wasn't either of you?" Liz asked. When they shook their heads, she continued on up to the third floor. Two sets of footsteps followed her.

At the top of the stairs, Liz bent double for a moment to catch her breath. Penny was standing in the doorway of her mother's bedroom, the Sunrise Room. "Come here!" she called, motioning wildly to Liz.

Liz hurried to the room, fearing what she was about to see. Louise had looked paler and more tired that morning at breakfast. Had she collapsed? Was she not as recovered from her recent heart surgery as Penny had hoped?

The sight that met her was unexpected, and the breath went out of her with a whoosh. Across the room, tiny Louise Rollins sat in a chair by the window, wrapped in her shawl and looking much calmer than her daughter.

"What happened?" Liz asked, ready to shake Penny for nearly giving *her* a heart attack.

"A miracle of sorts." Penny pointed to her mother's bed. Sitting right in the exact center of a round red pillow was an amber pill bottle.

"Is that what it looks like?" Liz asked.

"What is it?" Cherise and Viv called, trying to peer over Liz's shoulder.

"Mother's blood pressure medicine, the prescription that disappeared along with her makeup and jewelry." Penny flipped her long gray braid over her shoulder. "We got back an hour ago from picking up her new prescription. We were talking in my room, and then Mother came back here to change into her Watson costume. That's when she found the bottle."

Liz didn't touch the medicine bottle, wondering if there could be fingerprints on it that could be checked. She wished now that that had occurred to her with the reappearing knife too.

Liz squatted down beside Louise. "Did you leave your door unlocked while you were gone?"

"No, I locked it." Louise frowned, pulled her shawl closer, and leaned to whisper in Liz's ear. "At least, I'm almost certain I did."

Penny confirmed it. "It was still locked a few minutes ago when she came back to change."

"I don't know what to say," Liz said.

Vivian stepped into the room. "You mean it's not part of the mystery weekend, trying to keep us all guessing?"

"No, it's not. I meant it when I said the pickpocketing was just for fun and would only take place on the ground floor. I've had several pickpocketed items turned in already." She gazed around the Sunrise Room, with its wicker baskets and brightly colored pillows. There was no entrance to the room other than the door to the hallway and the third-floor window. Liz hated to do it, but it was probably time to involve the police and see what they advised.

Deep in thought, Liz descended the staircase much more slowly than she'd run up it. How had the medicine been returned with Louise's door locked? Liz had the master key and the only other extra keys for each bedroom.

So how had someone gained access to both Louise's and Cherise's rooms?

They must have forgotten to lock their doors when they left. A short trip across the landing to the bathroom on the third floor, or coming down for breakfast, or even visiting each other's rooms—any of those things could have left a room vulnerable to an intruder.

Liz sighed in frustration. Even if she kept her eyes sharp, she could only be in one place at a time. Where was a London constable when you had a *real* crime to report?

None of the so-called crimes even made sense to Liz. Someone was stealing, then returning some things but not others. Louise's belongings had been taken, but then her medicine was returned in plain sight, guaranteeing it would be found. Her jewelry hadn't reappeared, though. On the other hand, Cherise's necklace was removed, then returned, except it was so well hidden that few people would have found it. And Liz's own missing knife was returned in a very creepy way, ensuring that Liz would know she hadn't merely mislaid it.

She wasn't so sure she could file a formal police report now that some of the items had been returned.

Someone was toying with all of them. But who? And *why*?

9

By quarter to three, Liz was dressed in the royal blue Victorian day dress sewn by her friends. Pink ribbon trim aside, she felt as if she'd been transported back in time along with her guests and actors. As Liz passed the door of Sew Welcome, she saw several customers inside. They'd probably prevent Sadie from watching the next act.

By the time the Holmes/Watson pairs descended the staircase for Act Three, Liz had donned her most mysterious smile. *The show must go on.*

"Before we enter the Braithwaites' bedroom for Act Three, let me set the scene for you," she said. "It's now two days after James Braithwaite reported his rare Dickens edition stolen from his home. It's evening, and Mr. and Mrs. Braithwaite are in their bedroom." She opened the door to the sitting room and peeked in to make sure Jackson and Naomi were in place, then swung the door wide. "Please line up along the back wall for the best view."

The flames from the two candelabra flickered wildly in the draft from the door opening and closing, then straightened and burned brightly. Liz smiled. Using the candelabra instead of the electric chandelier for this scene had been the right choice for enhancing the ambiance.

When all the guests were situated, Liz nodded at the actors.

JAMES BRAITHWAITE: What a storm tonight! Did you hear the horses in the stables? Pure panic!

NETTIE BRAITHWAITE: Well, it's over, so there's nothing to disturb our sleep now.

JAMES: Not true. Storm or no storm, there's no excuse for the evening Globe *not being delivered.*

(There is a knock on the door, and Doyle enters.)

DOYLE: Your newspaper just arrived, sir. It's dampish. Shall I iron it?

JAMES: Not tonight. I'll read it as is.

(Doyle bows and retires to adjoining dressing room behind a screen.)

JAMES (unfolding the paper and scanning the front page): I say! This is a fine thing.

NETTIE (turning from where she is brushing her hair at the bureau): What is, dear?

JAMES: Godfrey.

NETTIE: Your publishing friend?

JAMES: Yes. He put the news of my reward on the front page. Good man. Now that's publishing sense. Good report. (He continues to read, lips moving, but his smile fades. Surprise shows, followed by outrage.) That swine, Liddle!

You can't trust the police or reporters. One of them must have my stolen Dickens.

NETTIE (*comes to stand by her husband*): Now calm down, James. Remember your heart.

JAMES: Calm down? But Nettie, listen to the description of my book. "*The stolen book by Charles Dickens,* Sketches by Boz, *was illustrated by George Cruikshank, with sixteen colored plates, including two frontispieces.*"

NETTIE (*frowning*): Is something amiss there?

JAMES (*throwing down the paper and storming about the bedroom*): I never told the constable that it had two frontispieces. Liddle could only know that if he had stolen the book or knew who did. He must have seen it.

NETTIE (*frowning*): Did the constable write the article?

JAMES (*slowly*): No.

NETTIE: Then perhaps the reporter added that detail on his own.

JAMES: Of course. The reporter has seen my book. He knows who has it.

NETTIE: What is a frontispiece?

JAMES: *It's a piece of art that faces the book's title page. It might be a portrait of the author or a beautiful painting. But I only told Liddle about the sixteen colored plates inside. I never mentioned the frontispieces.*

NETTIE: *What will you do?*

JAMES *(pacing back and forth across the bedroom):* *The publisher is responsible for whatever his reporter wrote. (Pacing more frantically.) Doyle!*

DOYLE *(appearing from the dressing room):* *Yes, sir?*

JAMES: *I'm getting dressed to go to Godfrey Denshaw's home right now. This can't wait till tomorrow.*

NETTIE: *Calm yourself, James. (Grabs his arm as he stomps past.) It's too late to bother him tonight.*

JAMES *(shaking off her hand):* *Don't try to stop me. Time is of the essence. (He suddenly clutches his dressing gown over his chest and gasps with pain.)*

NETTIE: *James? James! (She helps him to the bed, screaming.) Doyle, send for Dr. Fitzhugh! It's an emergency!*

Caught up in the drama, Liz almost forgot to step forward and announce, "Twenty minutes pass while Doyle sends a message to the village doctor."

A knock sounded on the door and Doyle answered it. David Mills, costumed in his doctor's black coat with tails and carrying a leather bag, stepped in and hurried to James Braithwaite's bedside.

JAMES (breathing heavily): I told her not to send for you.

DR. FITZHUGH: Your wife did the right thing. Now lie back.

JAMES: I need to see someone tonight. It's urgent.

DR. FITZHUGH (listening with stethoscope): Quiet, please. You're not going anywhere tonight, Mr. Braithwaite. Your heart is beating out of control. Very erratic.

JAMES: You don't understand. This can't wait.

DR. FITZHUGH (shaking his head): You must calm yourself.

NETTIE: That's what I keep telling him. James, you must guard your health. Remember, Andrew will be here in two days. (She turns to the doctor to explain.) Andrew is our son. He's been stationed in Africa, and we haven't seen him for two years.

DR. FITZHUGH: Listen to your wife, sir. You don't want to be laid up in the hospital when your son arrives.

(James lies back in bed, defeated. Nettie holds his hand.)

When the actors froze in place, Liz stepped forward. "This is the end of Act Three." She glanced at her watch. "Your five minutes start now."

Jeremy and Vivian wanted to see inside the doctor's bag and examine the stethoscope. Paul picked up the evening *Globe*, a copy of the front page that Liz had found online and tweaked, but it was empty inside. Penny and her mother peered behind the decorated screen that had blocked off Mr. Braithwaite's dressing room.

"Time's up," Liz said at the end of five minutes. "Take your clues and find a quiet place to discuss them. Although it's overcast this afternoon, it isn't supposed to snow, so the porch rockers are available too if you bundle up. Tea, coffee, and snacks are in the dining room if you want something hot to take outside." After all the guests filed out, she turned to the actors. "What drama this time! Great job, you guys."

While they discussed how the scene had gone, Liz put the sitting room to rights. *If only the drama this weekend was confined to the scripted acts.* Then she took the candelabra back to the dining room. Act Four that evening would be much less work for her. Set in a London publisher's office, Act Four only included the main character, James Braithwaite, and the newspaper publisher, Godfrey Denshaw, played by Rob Carver, Pleasant Creek's own newspaper reporter.

Liz returned to the rotunda as the actors shrugged into winter coats. "Liz, we're grabbing a bite for supper, but *not* at my bakery." Naomi pulled on fuzzy mittens. "Come with us?" She hooked her arms through those of Jackson and David. "You can get away for fried apple pies at Burger Heaven, can't you? Just for an hour?"

"Normally I'd jump at the chance," Liz said, "but with the mystery weekend, guests roam around the inn 'detecting' and need something a lot of the time."

Jackson looked disappointed, but then said, "Well, who knows? A fried apple pie might find its way here later."

Liz grinned. He'd remembered how much she loved them.

"What about you, Bert?" Naomi asked. "Butlers have to eat too."

"No can do," he replied. "I have a previous engagement."

David disentangled himself from Naomi. "I'll get something later." He turned to Liz. "If you don't mind, I'll hang around a bit and practice my part for Act Five tomorrow. I won't be in Act Four tonight."

"Sure, practice all you want. Act Five will be in the dining room."

"Our party sure shrank," Jackson commented as David and Bert left. "Can we help you with anything before we go?"

Liz thought a moment, checked the four-season room, and motioned her two friends to join her there.

"What is it?" Naomi asked. "More thefts?"

"Yes. And no." Liz explained about Cherise's necklace being stolen, but later returned and hidden in her room. "And Louise's medication was returned, but not *her* jewelry. And that's not all." She told them about David's odd behavior following Rhoda, and guests who wondered if the pickpocket was taking items from their rooms.

"Don't they lock their doors?" Jackson asked.

"I don't think they all were at first, unless they left the building to go eat, but I've asked them to."

Naomi tilted her head sideways. "It feels like someone is playing pranks, and they're certainly upsetting, but has something else happened?"

Liz hesitated. Putting it into words—especially if her friends were horrified by it—would mean she could no longer shrug it off. "There *was* something else," she said. And she told them about her missing knife that was returned, plunged into the melon up to the hilt. "What do you think it means?"

"I don't know," Jackson said slowly, "but I don't like it."

"I don't either." Naomi squeezed Liz's hand.

"I wish I hadn't washed the knife. There might have been fingerprints on it."

"Maybe." Jackson frowned. "But most people these days know enough to wipe things like that clean."

They discussed the eerie events for a few more minutes, until Liz heard staccato footsteps in the rotunda. She could already identify the sound. Resigned, she sighed and called, "Cherise? I'm in the four-season room."

Cherise clicked inside. "Well!" she cried, ignoring Liz's friends. "Did Watson solve any mysteries all by himself when Sherlock disappeared?"

Liz eyed her. "I don't understand. Is there a problem?"

"You might say so. It was—" She stopped, and Jackson and Naomi took their cue to leave.

"We'll talk later," Naomi said.

Even after Naomi and Jackson left, Cherise dropped her voice to a whisper. "It was humiliating enough to be stuck with the most unattractive person here." Her voice rose. "But Paul the Order-My-Own-Pizza man always plods off alone to think. Aren't we supposed to work together? He always wants to think by himself in his room. And I can't discuss the clues with anyone else."

Liz had to admit that she hadn't seen Paul and Cherise together except during the actual performances of the first three acts. She had assumed they'd disappeared to another ground floor room or even gone for a walk like the others.

"I'm sorry, Cherise. Did he mention why he was isolating himself?"

"No." She tossed her blonde mane. "I realize that he might be awestruck at being paired up with a movie star. It affects people that way sometimes. But he shouldn't let my fame intimidate him."

"Do you think that's the reason?" Liz asked, hoping her amusement was hidden.

"Actually, no." Cherise ran hands down the sides of the tight jeans she'd changed into. "I expect he's overwhelmed by the comparison between *his* age and size, and me being younger and well, *fit*, if you get my drift."

"That could certainly be the case." Liz wondered what it would be like to have such high self-esteem that it didn't occur to one that someone might be avoiding her because they didn't like her. "Are you sure he's just thinking in his room?" Liz asked. "Maybe he doesn't feel well."

Or—heaven help her—had her London food made him sick enough to retire to his room most of the day? She chided herself for not even noticing his absence. Liz laid a hand on Cherise's arm. "I'll run upstairs and check on him."

"I'll come with you."

"Let me go alone. If he's intimidated by you, he might be too embarrassed to say what's wrong."

"You're right." Cherise gave Liz a dismissive head-to-toe glance. "He shouldn't be intimidated by you."

Liz smiled at the backhanded compliment, chalking it up to another of her "how to survive and thrive as an innkeeper" rules. Upstairs, she knocked at the door of the Somewhere in Time Room and waited. She knocked again. A moment later a key turned in the lock. Liz blinked in surprise. It was unusual to have guests lock themselves in, other than at night.

"Oh, it's you." Paul stepped back to allow Liz to enter.

As much as his bulky size allowed, he scurried back to the desk, which was strewn with four or five papers torn from a Sherlock Holmes notepad. With some irritation, Liz noted that the desk had also been cleared of the three antique clocks that usually rested there.

When Paul grabbed a magazine to cover his notes, Liz hid her amusement. Why was he taking the solving of the crime so seriously? Did he think she would read his notes and tell the other sleuths his conclusions? And why was he working to solve it without the help of his partner?

"I wondered if you felt all right," Liz began, flinching at the stacked pizza boxes and empty soda cans. A half-eaten piece of cold pizza lay on top of a box, the edges of the pepperoni curling. She had to avert her eyes. "I hadn't seen you this weekend, other than breakfast and when the first three scenes were acted out." When he didn't respond, Liz pressed on. "Did my London breakfast upset your stomach?"

"Maybe. I wasn't expecting fried leftovers." He hiked up his drooping trousers and shook his shaggy hair back out of his eyes. "Do you have any liquid antacid medicine?"

"I'm afraid not. I do have some chewable tablets though."

"Liquid is the only kind that helps."

"Do you feel well enough to come downstairs and work with Cherise to solve the crime?"

"You can't discuss anything *with* her," he grumbled.

"Why not?"

He *humphed*. "She cuts you off, or she corrects you. She takes every single thing I say and turns it into a story about her so-called acting career. She doesn't really want to discuss the clues."

Liz remembered her own encounters with Cherise and privately agreed. "I'm sorry you and Cherise aren't more compatible," she finally said, "but the weekend was advertised as teaming up with another guest. I couldn't guarantee that you'd hit it off."

He nodded grudgingly.

"If you can, Paul, please go over your clues with Cherise for fifteen or twenty minutes before Act Four tonight." At his reluctant nod, she smiled. "I do appreciate it."

Coming downstairs, Liz gave Cherise a fifty-fifty chance that

Paul would spend time with her to work out the clues. She hoped that he only felt out of his league, and he wasn't ignoring Cherise to knock her down a peg or two. Granted, she could be annoying, but Liz had a sneaking suspicion that the starlet wasn't nearly as self-confident as she tried to project.

As Liz fixed a couple of loose London posters, David emerged from the dining room. "All ready for tomorrow?" she asked. "You did great in Act Three."

"Thanks. It's been fun. But I should head out. I'm subbing for someone on the night shift tonight."

"I don't know how you do it," Liz said. "After a long day's work, I'm ready to drop. I don't think I could work a night shift too."

"It's mostly prep work for tomorrow, so it should be an easy night."

Liz walked with him to the front door and stepped out on the porch. "I love taking a minute outside at the end of the day." Dusk was quickly approaching. She loved Pleasant Creek at this time of day. The quiet. The calm. The twinkling lights coming on in various shops. The rustle of wind blowing the dried leaves still clinging to the oak trees. And, like right now, the *clip-clop* of horses' hooves on the cobblestone street.

Saturday was a busy time in town. She hoped some of her guests had shopped at the weekend market that afternoon. It was held in a large empty store, not outside at this time of year, but it was always well attended. People came from miles around to buy Amish crafts and homemade baked goods.

A horse-drawn buggy passed in front of the inn then, and Liz squinted in the dim light. Unless she was mistaken, the driver was Rhoda, the Amish woman who created the faceless dolls. A younger woman sat on the bench seat beside her. Whoever it was, Liz hoped she'd sold everything she brought with her to market today.

She waved David off and had just stepped foot inside when a car shot from behind the buggy, drove within inches of the horse, and ran the buggy off the road. The light-colored car hurtled at high speed on down the road without stopping. Liz stared in horror.

The horse reared and started to bolt. Liz shouted, but David was already running into the street. He grabbed the horse by its harness and pulled its head down. From the porch, Liz heard his soothing murmurs, talking calmly until the jumpy horse stood still. Then, still gripping the harness, he led the horse back onto the road, the buggy jouncing behind over the concrete edge of the street. After speaking for a moment to the woman holding the reins, David stepped back and waved. The buggy continued down the road at a steady, measured pace.

Liz ran to the street. "That was brave of you," she said. "You could have been trampled."

"The horse was just frightened." He peered down the road. "Did you happen to notice that car's license plate?"

"No, it happened too fast. It was just some light-colored four-door." Liz shook her head. She couldn't believe what she'd witnessed. Accidents rarely happened with drivers not seeing the Amish buggies, even at dusk. However, unless her eyes had deceived her, that was no accident. Liz would have sworn that the side-swiping was deliberate. The accident could have been so much worse.

"I'm glad everyone's okay." With a wave of his long arm, he headed off down the street.

Liz watched him for a moment, grateful that David had been in the right place at the right time to stop the panicked horse from bolting and overturning the buggy. Heading up the sidewalk to the inn, she rubbed her cold arms and wondered how David had become so adept and skilled with horses. He was a man with hidden talents.

What else was David hiding?

10

Back inside, Liz darted into her private quarters and closed the door. She fixed a cup of apple cinnamon tea, curled up on her sofa with an afghan tucked around her, and relaxed for ten minutes by reading a few pages of the novel she was currently enjoying. If only she could stay curled up there for an hour or two. But duty called.

While resting, she'd vaguely heard doors opening and closing, and she hoped all six of her guests had gone somewhere for supper. They were lucky to have eating places within walking distance, plus the bakery next door. The grocery store nearby also stocked favorite Amish foods, from sourdough bread and pies to homemade butter and cheeses.

Before she fixed a sandwich for her supper, Liz hurried through the ground floor. She straightened magazines in the sitting room, cleaned the never-ending crumbs from the sideboard in the dining room, and rearranged furniture in the library so setting up for Act Four would go quickly.

Grabbing a pillow off the library couch, she discovered a brown leather book stashed behind it. It wasn't a book from her shelves. After finding no name on the flyleaf, she flipped through a few pages and realized it was a journal. It must belong to one of the guests. She was tempted to read it and find out if this particular Holmes/Watson team was on the right track in figuring out the solution.

As she was closing the journal, a phrase underlined in red jumped out at her. She reopened the diary and read, *I'm so afraid!* Her heart skipped a beat when she noticed, on the adjoining page, another sentence underlined in red: *How will I survive all alone?*

Liz closed the journal abruptly, debating what to do. A person certainly wouldn't want this personal journal left lying around for the others to read. Why had it been stashed there? Had a guest hidden it when unexpectedly interrupted, intending to come back for it?

Pondering what to do, Liz decided to tuck it out of sight in her living quarters. Within half an hour, cheery voices drifted from the sitting room, and Liz carried in a fresh tray of mugs and homemade cherry-almond granola bars, depositing them near the single-cup coffee brewer.

As she assisted with the coffee and tea, Liz enjoyed viewing the purchases her guests had made in various shops when out for supper. Penny had purchased a beautiful set of heart-shaped ceramic bowls from Cracked Pots, the artisan gallery at the edge of town. Louise had found a book on Amish quilts at Pleasant Creek's bookstore, Once Upon a Tale. Jeremy had purchased cheesecake at Mama's Home Cooking and declared it the best he'd ever had.

Liz looked down and spotted a small box on the floor by Vivian's feet. It held four faceless Amish dolls: two parents, a boy, and a girl. "What made you buy the Amish doll family?" Liz asked.

Vivian nodded, ducking her head sheepishly. "I saw a flyer for a big craft fair held at a church." She held up one of the child dolls. "I find them fascinating. It makes you wonder what they're thinking."

Jeremy guffawed, and Vivian colored.

Liz jumped in. "You're so right, Vivian. I think they're lovely." She and Vivian talked about the various ways the dolls were made and why they were so plain.

As Penny and her mother gathered their purchases to leave, Liz remembered the journal. "Say, before any of you go, I found a brown leather journal that was left in the library. Does it belong to any of you?"

Penny glanced up, startled. "It's mine. I'm glad you found it."

"If you come with me, I'll get it. It's in my private quarters for safekeeping."

"Mother, wait here," Penny said. "I'll be back to get you in a minute."

In her quarters, Liz handed Penny the journal. "Yes, it's mine," she said, avoiding Liz's eyes.

"I imagine you meant to come back for it, but—"

"No. I mean, I didn't leave my diary anywhere except my bedroom." Liz's heart sank. *Not again.* "Someone removed it from your room?"

"They must have." Penny sighed. She reached out and touched Liz's arm. "But it's not what you're thinking."

And to Liz's amazement, tears welled in Penny's eyes.

"Here, sit down." Liz guided Penny to her couch and handed her a tissue.

"I'm sorry." Penny took a deep breath and wiped her eyes.

Liz waited, not wanting to push, but eager to know if her own mystery of the stolen items was about to be solved. The silence grew. Penny slouched, head down, her thick gray braid hanging by her face. She shredded her tissue into strips.

Liz handed her the tissue box. "If you didn't take your journal from your room, and you don't think someone else took it, then how do you account—"

"I'm sure Mother took my diary and left it downstairs. I only hope she didn't read it."

Liz remained silent.

"Mother is my last living relative," Penny finally said. "I started keeping a diary six months ago when the doctor diagnosed her with dementia. I needed a place to dump my feelings, to write about my fear of being alone."

"Penny, I'm so sorry. I had no idea." Liz patted her back. "I do understand how hard it is to lose a mother."

"I've always lived with Mother—I never married—and I have little social life. We've always been close." Penny looked up then, her eyes red rimmed and haunted. "Mother's heart surgery six weeks ago made me face that I would lose her someday. Before her surgery, she made out her will. That brought the finality of it all into sharp focus."

Liz went to get Penny a glass of water. As she sipped, she mentioned signs she'd noticed that her mother was experiencing more "mental slippage." Louise couldn't remember her own birthday one day. Another day she'd gone to visit a neighbor but had gotten lost on the walk home. As Penny talked, Liz remembered a couple of instances herself. One in particular stood out—Louise had asked her daughter if she, Louise, disliked barking dogs. It had seemed odd at the time that she couldn't remember her own likes and dislikes.

Penny's voice was monotone as she listed one incident after another. "Mother's belongings turn up in some odd places sometimes—money under her pillow, a watch in a coat pocket, or postage stamps in a vase of flowers." She sighed and raised her eyes to Liz. "And I have a confession to make. I think that Mother's missing jewelry and toiletries are things she's misplaced herself. I won't file an insurance report or anything, but after the weekend is over, you might find the jewelry hidden in the inn somewhere, like you found my diary. If you do, could you mail it to us? It's not worth much money, but it has sentimental value."

"I understand. So you think she mislaid her own medicine, and then found it again?"

"Nothing else makes sense."

Liz wished that were entirely true. But what about Cherise's stolen necklace that had been returned? And Liz's own knife that had been buried up to its hilt in the melon? To Liz, that bordered on being mentally unbalanced, more than forgetful. Could those incidents be attributed to the gentle Louise?

Liz kept her tone gentle. "I wish you had been more forthcoming about Louise's condition, even though she's in the early stages. I think the other guests should know about it."

"Please don't. I want everyone to treat her normally."

"I need to consider all my guests though. And remember, you're in a strange house, an inn with three floors and a dozen rooms. Louise could easily get confused about which room is hers. She might even open a wrong door and end up outside with no coat in freezing temperatures. If the others knew of her condition, they could look out for her." *And lock their doors from now on.*

"I hadn't thought of that." Penny nodded. "You make sense, but I don't want Mother to hear you tell them."

"Naturally." Liz thought a moment. "Go take Louise upstairs to dress in her costume for Act Four. While you do that, I'll tell the others. I do think it's best."

Penny nodded, wiped her eyes again, and left. Liz watched her go, pondering their conversation. Then, seemingly out of nowhere, a suspicion reared its ugly head. Was it possible that Penny had planted the journal for someone to find, that she *wanted* everyone to know about her mother? Liz tossed the idea around in her mind. It was possible, she admitted. Penny wouldn't be the first person Liz had known who basked in the reputation of a martyr.

Before heading back to the dining room, Liz climbed the stairs and knocked on the Somewhere in Time door. "Paul? Can you join the others in the sitting room for a short, but important, meeting?" She was surprised how quickly he complied.

In the sitting room, she summarized what she'd learned and stressed Penny's desire that they treat Louise normally. "I would like to add that, whenever you're around Louise, be aware in case she wanders outside without a coat, for example. I think we can be helpful without hovering or making it obvious." She looked from one guest to another. "Any questions before you go change to watch Act Four?"

Jeremy, who was already wearing his deerstalker hat, stood as if to make a speech. "I, for one, don't believe that daughter's story. What's her name? Penny? In fact, I think it's despicable that she's exploiting her own mother. What if she's stealing things herself and using her mother as a cover? Then if her dotty mother is blamed, she'll be excused because of dementia. And Penny gets away scot-free."

"Jeremy, you have a good imagination, but that kind of talk isn't helpful." Liz tried to keep the edge out of her voice. "That's pure speculation, and we don't need that." No one spoke for a minute. Finally, Liz said, "Are there any more questions or comments?"

Cherise gazed at each of the guests in turn, one eye hidden by the blonde hair carefully draped over her face. Then, when everyone was focused on her, she flung her long hair in a whirl over her shoulder. "I once played a caregiver for a dementia patient. Did any of you see that movie?" The others shrugged and shook their heads. Cherise sighed audibly. "Well, I conducted an extensive study of dementia for that part—you know, to immerse myself in the character—and in my opinion, that skinny Louise doesn't have any such disease."

Jeremy jumped back in. "Skinny Louise seems fine to me too. Who knows? Maybe the daughter goes to B&Bs all over the country and pulls this 'my poor demented mother the kleptomaniac' scam." The corners of his mouth tilted upward smugly. "Hey, that could be my next plot."

Liz couldn't think of a thing to say. This whole weekend had gone totally out of control.

Vivian cleared her throat and, for the first time, pulled away from the mystery writer. "I think we should do what Liz asked and keep an eye out for Louise."

Paul linked his fingers over his round stomach, watching Vivian with both surprise and appreciation. "I agree. I had two grandparents with dementia, and it's not a joke. And it doesn't look the same in everyone."

"Thank you," Liz said, thankful for his support. "And now, you might want to retire to your rooms to dress in your costumes for Act Four. It will start promptly at seven."

While the guests filed from the room, Liz heard Sadie close up shop for the night. Liz yearned to do the same thing. At that point, she didn't think she'd ever do another mystery weekend. She'd already gotten more than she bargained for. In the kitchen, she sat at her desk and reviewed her checklist for the rest of the day.

But instead of Sadie going outside, she popped into the kitchen. "Got a second?" she asked, breathless.

"Sure. What's up?" Liz asked.

"Mary Ann had an accident."

"Oh no!" Liz jumped up. "A car accident?"

"No, she was playing soccer."

Liz abruptly sat back down. "Soccer?" Then light dawned. "With the grandkids?"

"Got it in one." Sadie demonstrated a swift soccer kick. "Apparently she was in the backyard with the three boys, getting them to work off some steam."

"Did she fall?" Liz asked.

"No, but she rolled her ankle in a divot in her yard and has a pretty bad sprain. She can barely hobble around, she said, and with the boys spending the night, she needs help." Sadie consulted her scribbled list. "I'm supposed to pick up a couple of movies, some video games, and three pizzas, then head over to Mary Ann's."

"Can the parents be called back? Or what about Howard? Where's he?"

"If her husband was working in the university lab or the library, she'd call him home, but he's off speaking at a conference somewhere. And I doubt Mary Ann will call the boys' parents either. It's an anniversary overnight, and Mary Ann won't want to spoil it for them."

"Tell Mary Ann I hope she feels better soon."

"Will do. I'll stay overnight if she'll let me. I'm just sorry we can't help you the rest of this weekend. We were both looking forward to it."

"I understand." Liz gave Sadie a hug. "You're a good friend. If my hands weren't tied with this event, I'd go help too."

"She knows you would. Not to worry." She zipped up her parka. "Better go before the natives get too restless."

Back in her private quarters after Sadie left, Liz couldn't settle down. Pacing back and forth, she finally came to a decision and picked up her phone. Although David wasn't scheduled to perform again until Sunday, this couldn't wait.

"David? Hi. It's Liz. Can you talk?"

"Just for a minute. My break's almost over."

"Sorry. I forgot you were working an extra shift."

"Not a problem. What can I do for you?"

Liz chose her words with care. "I don't want you to do any more pickpocketing. It didn't work out like I'd hoped. Someone might be taking advantage of the mystery weekend to steal things. Or one of our guests, Louise, has dementia as her daughter claims and is moving and losing things. Either way, something that was supposed to be a fun 'extra' has gone awry."

The line was quiet.

"David? You still there?"

"Do you suspect *me* of taking advantage this weekend to steal things?" The hurt tone was unmistakable.

"No, of course not."

"I only took things from their pockets, and I only did it on the main floor. I've turned in everything to you that I pickpocketed."

"I believe you." *Mostly.* "I'll see you tomorrow for Act Five at eleven o'clock."

"I'll be there. G'night."

Liz tossed her phone on her bed and noticed Beans standing in her doorway. She knelt on the rug and opened her arms. He nestled there with such a contented look that Liz suspected he might purr. "I wish I'd chosen someone else to play the doctor," she murmured into his fur, "someone I've known longer." David had seemed like such an answer to her prayers at the time. Now she wasn't so sure.

11

When Liz opened the door at six thirty, she simply stared. "I hardly recognized you, Rob. Come on in."

Jackson ran up the front steps and followed Rob through the door. Liz was relieved that they were in plenty of time for the performance of Act Four.

She closed the door against a sharp wind that had picked up, then turned to get a closer look at Rob Carver. With his red hair and freckles, the newspaper reporter for *Pleasant Creek News & Views* had always reminded Liz of an overgrown Tom Sawyer. But not tonight. He'd been transformed into a middle-aged man. He looked perfect for the part of the newspaper publisher now.

Liz studied his face up close. "Who did your makeup?"

"Rita at the playhouse. She used powdery stuff to turn my hair gray, and she drew some forehead creases with a grease pencil and even gave me a bit of padding." He patted his stomach. "I figured the publisher of a successful newspaper should look well fed."

"Well, you both look great." Liz sniffed appreciatively. "And what's that wonderful smell?"

"Could it possibly be a fried apple pie from Burger Heaven?" Jackson asked.

"You didn't."

"I did." He grinned, pulling the bag from behind his back and holding it out.

"Don't tempt me. That will be my treat for later."

"Should I stash it in the kitchen?"

"That'd be great. Just be sure it's out of Beans's reach. In fact, you can wait in the kitchen until the guests are in the library. Rob, you'll already be in the library acting as the publisher, but I want the guests to see Braithwaite's dramatic entrance. I'll motion when it's time for Jackson to enter."

"Roger." Swinging the fragrant Burger Heaven paper sack, Jackson disappeared into her kitchen.

Liz smiled to herself. Amazing how a fried apple pie from Burger Heaven could brighten a person's night. Or was it more the delivery boy who'd done that? "Come into the library, Rob, and get in place before the guests arrive."

The library was now a London publisher's office. Liz had tacked up posters of Victorian newspapers' front pages, stacked a few library books on each available surface, and strewn papers across the desk. Other touches, like her old inkwell and a sign pointing to the typesetter's room, were icing on the cake. She lit candles around the room.

"Where should I stand?" Rob asked.

"Behind the desk," Liz said, pointing. "Here's a photocopy of an old London paper, the morning *Globe*. When the guests come in at first, you'll be alone, reading the front page of the paper that's hot off your own printing press." She scanned the articles. "Choose a couple of them to read under your breath. Jackson will burst into your office very soon, so react with surprise when he does."

"Got it."

Back in the rotunda, Liz waited in her own Victorian dress for all the Sherlocks and Watsons to gather in front of the closed library door. Hopefully Jeremy and Cherise had had time to reconsider their harsh opinions about Penny. If not, surely they would at least have the good grace to keep quiet around her. As soon as Paul came down—last to join them, as always—Liz cleared her throat.

"Tonight is Act Four. It is the morning after James Braithwaite read the newspaper article about his reward offer that so disturbed him. Only the newspaper publisher, Godfrey Denshaw, is in his office, perusing the front page of his newspaper, the morning *Globe*."

Liz ushered the six guests into the room. Glancing at her sideways, she studied Louise, who seemed the same as usual, dressed in her Dr. Watson costume and covered by her ever-present shawl. After they arranged themselves at the back of the room, Liz shut the library door and nodded at Rob to begin.

GODFREY DENSHAW (standing at desk, muttering as he scans that day's headlines aloud, nodding as if pleased): 'Be Systematic,' 'Advice to a Young Lawyer,' 'Bristol Woman Denounced by Teetotalers.' Excellent, excellent.

The door flew open, and Godfrey jerked his head up to gaze in astonishment at the newcomer.

JAMES BRAITHWAITE (entering, with top hat in his left hand): Godfrey, just the man I want to see.

GODFREY (coming around in front of desk to shake hands): What are you doing out on the streets so early? Come to bring the reward money?

JAMES: I want to talk to the reporter who wrote the story of my book theft.

GODFREY: You want to thank him? No wonder. He did a bang-up job. You could get it back today. If it's returned here,

I'll send it right over. (Laughs.) After I look at it again first.

JAMES: I want to talk to that reporter personally, do you understand?

GODFREY: Are you giving him a reward as well? Commendable!

JAMES: Not a reward. I want to ask him how he learned about the frontispieces mentioned in his article. I made no mention of them in my report to the constable.

GODFREY: Odd. Well, he's on his beat now, but I'll get a message to him when he comes in. Won't be for hours though. (He walks behind desk, sits, and pulls paper and ink toward himself.) Say, how's that son of yours?

JAMES: Exciting news. Andrew is coming home from Africa in two days, on the Indian Queen. We haven't seen him in two years. Nettie is beside herself with planning for his homecoming.

GODFREY: How long will he be home this time?

JAMES: Permanently, we hope. He plans to resettle in London. (He replaces his top hat on his head.) I see you're busy. I'll be off, but send that reporter to see me the very minute he arrives.

After Jackson left the room, Liz stepped forward. "Remember, only five minutes to make your observations."

Four of the sleuths pored over the newspapers on the desk and the wall, pointing and taking notes. Penny and Louise hung back, though, and when Liz looked closer, she saw tears running down Louise's wrinkled cheeks. Long skirt rustling, Liz moved near them. "Should we go out in the hall?" she whispered.

At Penny's urgent nod, Liz ushered them out the door and into the sitting room. "Can I help?"

Penny held her mother's thin hand. "Who played the newspaper publisher?"

"Rob Carver. He works for our local newspaper."

"Mother was struck—as I was—by the similarity between the actor and my brother. He left home years ago and never returned. The likeness was uncanny."

Louise silently twisted the ends of her shawl around her finger, almost as if Penny's words didn't register.

"I'm so sorry to hear that," Liz said. The poor woman. While it hadn't been intentional, Liz regretted stirring up painful memories for Louise. This was supposed to be a celebration weekend for them, a time to have fun after her frightening heart surgery. Liz glanced at her watch. *How many other things can go wrong this weekend?* "Stay in here as long as you like. I'll make this room off-limits to the others for now." She paused. "Let me know if there's anything I can do."

And with a sympathetic smile, she left to tell the others that their five minutes were up.

Liz gathered the remaining four guests outside the library door and was surprised to see Penny and Louise join them. "If you'd like to stay in a Sherlock and Watson mood," Liz said, "tonight I plan to show the movie *The Hound of the Baskervilles*. There's a flat-screen TV behind the cabinet doors in the library."

"Mother?" Penny asked. "Would you enjoy watching a Sherlock Holmes movie tonight?"

Louise looked considerably better, but she shook her head. "I'd like an early evening. But you watch if you like."

"No, I could use an early evening myself. Good night, all," Penny said.

The Rollinses started up the staircase, and Paul followed them, breathing heavily, but without a word or backward glance. Liz took that as a "no" as well.

Cherise did an elegant stretch. "I need my beauty sleep, so I'll pass on the movie too." She waited expectantly— poised for someone to express disappointment, Liz guessed—but no such comment was made. In fact, if anything, Vivian was having difficulty hiding her delight at Cherise's announcement. The idea of being curled up on the couch alone with Jeremy apparently didn't cause her undue concern.

"You see," Cherise continued, answering a question no one had asked, "my beauty routines require a couple of hours every single night before I can retire." She paused again. "A mask, steaming my pores, keeping my smile dazzling—all that takes time." She bestowed on them a blinding smile and then sashayed upstairs.

Liz raised an eyebrow at the remaining team. "How about you two? Are you in the mood for a scary movie on the moors?"

Vivian jumped in before Jeremy could take a breath. "We'd love to see it. Maybe while we watch Sherlock solve the mystery, his thinking process will rub off on us."

"It might. I'll straighten the library and then start the movie." Five minutes later, the movie, starring her favorite Sherlock actor, Jeremy Brett, was underway. Since her guests had turned down buttered popcorn, Liz was free for a bit.

She heaved a sigh of relief in her private quarters, grateful to change into something looser than her cinched-in Victorian skirt. Originally she'd hoped that Jackson would stay a while after Act Four, but he'd left with Rob. He had a late meeting with a customer at the store to pick up an anniversary gift, a custom dining set. However, as she relaxed in peace and quiet with a cup of tea and a slice of apple pie, she had to admit that it was heavenly to be alone for a bit.

While she waited for the movie to finish, Liz moved methodically down her to-do list. She finished the prep work for her revamped Sunday morning Victorian breakfast, precooking part of it. She cleaned up the dining room and sitting room so they would be ready in the morning. She even had fifteen minutes to read before the movie was over.

When she heard Vivian and Jeremy head upstairs during the credits, Liz made short work of returning the DVD to its case and turning off the lights. When she left the room, she could hear Vivian's and Jeremy's voices echoing down the stairwell. They must have been standing next to the banister on the second floor. Liz went to lock the front door, and when she returned, Jeremy was boasting that all the odd people at the Sherlock weekend had given him ideas for his next project. "In fact," Jeremy said, "a mystery weekend is the perfect chance to hide a real crime."

Vivian gave a girlish squeal. "I never thought of that. How clever!"

Liz perked up at that comment. With the inn so quiet at this time of night, Jeremy and Vivian might as well be talking five feet away. So her mystery weekend was the perfect time to hide a genuine crime? Was Jeremy inadvertently admitting that he was behind the odd thefts that weekend?

"Can you keep a secret?" Jeremy's voice lowered so that Liz had to strain to hear.

"Of course I can," Vivian said. "Absolutely."

He lowered his volume a bit more. "I'm not actually working on my next book. I'm writing a reality show to pitch to the networks. My agent loves the script so far."

"A reality show? How exciting!"

"That's why this weekend has been such a gold mine. That mindless Cherise would be great in a reality show, and she'd jump at the chance. She has no idea how ridiculous she appears. She's exactly the narcissistic type the TV producers want."

"Can I help publicize it? All you have to do is ask. I'll give you my list of contacts, anything that would help," Viv gushed.

Jeremy gave a self-deprecating chuckle. "I'll let you know when the time comes. Right now I have to finish it so my agent can pitch it. I have ideas for two episodes, but I need at least one more."

Liz tiptoed away from the staircase and Jeremy's dreams of television success. What a long and challenging day. Surely tomorrow would be better.

If nothing else, the guests were scheduled to leave before two o'clock, so even if it wasn't better, it would be *shorter*.

She hoped.

12

Liz awoke Sunday morning, her mood considerably brightened. Even with the curtains drawn, she could tell that it was a bright and sunny November morning. After some quiet devotional time in her room, she was ready to face the day.

She had higher hopes for today's London breakfast—a meat pudding, along with porridge and treacle syrup. To be on the safe side this time though, Liz also cut up some fresh fruit, even though Victorian Londoners would have had very little fresh fruit in November. She was carrying the ceramic bowl to the dining room when she heard an odd noise coming down the stairs. When she returned to get the orange juice and plates, the noise had risen to a wail, followed by frantic pounding.

Unless her ears deceived her, the voice belonged to Louise Rollins.

Liz pivoted and raced up the staircase. On the second floor, the crying was louder, and Vivian stepped outside the Heirloom Room. Liz motioned for her to stay there while she continued up to the third floor.

At the top of the stairs, Louise stood outside her daughter's bedroom door. Her blonde and silver braid, usually wound around her crown, hung limply down her back. Penny wrapped her arms around her mother's shaking body. "Mother? What's the matter? It's all right. I'm here."

Liz stopped a few feet away, not wanting to scare Louise, but she leaned close to hear her words.

"I saw someone outside my door! He was dressed in black."

"When?" Penny glanced around the top floor landing.

Liz darted toward the bathroom door and flung it open. No one was there. She even checked the shower. Not a soul.

"I want to go home," Louise whimpered.

"Mother, how did you see him? Did you open your door?"

"I watched him through the keyhole. He was staring right at me." She sagged against Penny's shoulder, and her daughter held her tight. "I want to go home," Louise repeated, her voice muffled.

"Pssst!"

Liz turned to see Vivian and Cherise appear at the top of the stairs. Cherise crooked a finger, motioning Liz closer. Dressed in high-heeled slippers and a chiffon robe, her hair was mussed and lipstick smeared. "Someone was up here yesterday too," she whispered. "I saw that guy who plays the doctor in your skits coming down from the third floor. He had no business being up here, did he?"

"I don't know." Though she was disturbed by the information about David, Liz kept her facial expression neutral. "I'll ask him about it. I'm sure there's a logical explanation." *At least, I hope there is.*

Liz glanced over Cherise's shoulder to find the remaining guests assembled on the steps just below her. Even Paul had come out of hiding to investigate the commotion. Snippets of contentious murmurings floated up the stairs.

"This makes me nervous," Cherise said. "And I *did* see that actor up here yesterday."

"Should we leave?" Vivian whispered.

"Nah, this is good theatrical stuff," Jeremy said. "Grist for the writing mill."

"I'm not going anywhere," Paul said. "If you all leave, then I win the prize by default."

"What prize?" Vivian's voice rose. "Is there a prize for solving the mystery?"

"I think we should *all* leave," Cherise said, "and get our money back too. I bet Louise will now."

Liz winced at that comment, but stopped herself from replying. She didn't want the weekend to end like this. For one thing, it would mean a big financial loss if they all demanded a refund for their rooms. She'd also spent money on the special food she'd cooked and paid a lot to rent costumes. Plus the resulting bad word-of-mouth publicity could cost her business later.

Once Penny's mother was calmer, Liz headed down the stairs, arms spread wide as if shooing chickens. "Let's go downstairs," she said. "All of you, come down to the dining room for breakfast while it's hot." She paused on the second-floor landing. "Wait until we've talked before you make up your minds about leaving or staying. I'd hate to see you leave before the final act at eleven this morning."

She hurried to the kitchen, where the meat pudding had simmered for two hours already. She lifted it out of the water and let it rest. Later it would be sliced and served with a thick, rich gravy. Porridge bubbled in a pot on the stove. It would be served with two kinds of treacle: a golden pale syrup, and a darker variety known as black treacle, or molasses, which had a strong, slightly bitter flavor that Sadie loved.

By the time she'd put everything on the dining room sideboard, all six guests were seated at the table. Liz was surprised to see Louise walk in, but she was neatly dressed—including an ivory shawl with fringe this time—and Liz took her appearance as a good sign.

Perhaps the second-floor guests had made an agreement amongst themselves not to ask Louise about her frightening experience. Whatever the reason, no one brought it up. Most likely Penny had asked them not to.

So far, so good.

Liz left to make more coffee, but hesitated outside the door, out of sight of the guests. It wasn't long before the grumbling started. The comments went from "What's in this meat pudding?" and "I bet the people in the workhouses ate better meals than this porridge" to "Treacle? It's just molasses, and it makes me gag." Only Vivian praised anything, saying that the dough and gravy of the meat pudding was "filling." *Faint praise.*

Liz knew she couldn't hesitate this time. If these mystery weekend guests weren't happily fed another day, they'd pack up and leave early. At the very least, several would ask for their money back or post rotten reviews online.

In the kitchen, she set Plan B in motion. She cracked a dozen eggs. While they scrambled, she fried some bacon. She'd found long ago that it was a very rare customer who wasn't thrilled and comforted by bacon. She hurried to the dining room, placed the extra dishes directly on the table, and pretended that she hadn't heard their earlier comments.

She gave them a bright smile. "I thought it would be nice to have some breakfast foods you were used to as well this morning. In two minutes, I'll have warm coffee cake for you." She was heartened by the immediately brightened faces around the table.

Before anyone could comment, she ran out the front door instead and next door to the Sweet Everything bakery. She wanted everyone to leave her table satisfied.

In five minutes, she was back with two coffee cakes: caramel-apple and blackberry-peach. She cut them and arranged squares on serving platters. She added them to the dining room table, then grabbed the dish of home-churned Amish butter from the sideboard and set it between the platters. "More coffee, anyone?" Liz asked brightly.

"Yes please." Jeremy tapped his cup.

Penny and Vivian nodded too, and she soon emptied the small pot. "I'll be back with more in a moment."

Back in the kitchen, Liz leaned briefly against the counter and breathed a sigh of relief. Unless she missed her guess, she'd just averted a mass exodus of her guests. If she somehow managed to keep them happy a few more hours, the extra effort required to make the expanded breakfast would be repaid in spades.

Just a while longer, she encouraged herself. *You can do this. Take one hour at a time.*

Liz felt terrible thinking it, but she couldn't wait for this weekend to be over. The usual guest chores were second nature to her now, but she'd misjudged how much additional work the mystery weekend would entail. Overseeing the "acting scenes" so they ran smoothly, redecorating different rooms for each new scene, creating her authentic breakfasts, and being at the constant beck and call of her demanding guests had nearly drained her reserves of peace and patience.

Liz was making more coffee when she turned to find Cherise, still in her high-heeled and feathered pink slippers, sail into the kitchen, her silky robe fanning out behind her like a pink bridal veil.

"Yes?" Liz asked. "What can I get for you?"

"Oh, nothing. I had a slice of melon and some coffee, but everything else is too loaded with calories for my figure." She patted her flat stomach.

Liz waited, but Cherise seemed to have forgotten why she was there. "Did you have a question about today's events?"

"Yes," Cherise said, "I have a couple questions, but not about that." She perched on a kitchen chair, crossed her legs, and carefully draped the chiffon robe to reveal a well-toned and well-tanned thigh. "I haven't had enough time to shadow you this weekend. I still need that first-hand information about the life of an innkeeper."

Liz smiled wanly, then turned back to wipe the counter and gather up the fruit rinds in the sink. "As you can see, it's an exciting life," she said over her shoulder.

"Oh, I won't be doing mundane things like this in the movie," Cherise assured her. "I was thinking about the unusual things. Like, how often do you have to deal with weird guests like Louise?"

Liz paused to make sure her reply wasn't sharp. "I get people with all kinds of stories and from different walks of life. It interests me, and I learn a lot. Being an innkeeper mostly involves showing kindness to people. For example, if you—"

"Well, what *I* would do is send her packing." Cherise waved her manicured nails in front of her. "In my last movie, before I was kidnapped, there was this girl who was a lunatic, I mean, truly certifiable . . ."

Liz let her ramble on as she loaded the dishwasher and swept the floor, and by then the new coffee was finished. Getting more creamer from the fridge, Liz carried it back to the dining room, with Cherise blathering and flapping her slippers right behind her all the way.

As she poured more coffee, Liz was relieved to discover that the guests had all decided to complete the mystery weekend over fresh coffee cake, bacon, and eggs.

Even Louise and Penny were staying and had decided to attend an early service at Pleasant Creek Community Church. "We'll be back in plenty of time for Act Five."

After everyone dispersed, Liz disappeared into the sitting room and curled up in a chair near the window. It wasn't even nine thirty yet, and she felt as if she'd run a marathon. The guests' differing personalities were nothing like the happy clue seekers she'd envisioned when she planned the weekend. Not to mention the stress of the events she *hadn't* planned.

Mentally, she shook herself. No need to borrow more trouble. Things had straightened out this morning, and she just needed to relax. With that in mind, she grabbed her boots and parka from the utility room and strode down toward the lake. If anything could de-stress her, this would.

She didn't have time to hike far, but she followed the trail by the lake around the first bend, grateful for the solitude.

But when she emerged through the weeping willow trees and turned a corner, she caught movement in her peripheral vision, broke her stride, and nearly tripped. She was surprised to discover she wasn't alone at the lake. Two people stood near the frozen water's edge, close but not touching. Their voices were pitched so low she couldn't distinguish the words.

Before they noticed her, she backed up to leave, but not before her mind registered that one of them was David. The other figure was an Amish woman, although the woman's *Kapp* obscured her face. What were they doing there together?

Liz shivered in the icy wind and pulled the quilted hood of her parka closer around her head as she snuck away.

Why did David's behavior always raise more questions than it answered?

13

Plowing diagonally across her snowy backyard, Liz pondered what in the world David was doing, meeting an Amish woman in a secluded area down at the lake. Could the woman have been Rhoda, whom he'd followed yesterday and had saved when her buggy had been forced off the road? Liz didn't know if she had the right to ask him about his clandestine meeting or not. It really was none of her business.

On the other hand, something else *was* her business. What had he been doing up on the third floor of the inn when she'd expressly told him to stay on the ground floor? Was David a genuine thief, not just her pretend pickpocket?

Or was it one of her guests? There was Jeremy, whose career had floundered—he could easily need valuables to pawn. Or was it Paul? Was he really reclusive because he didn't want to interact with Cherise? Or did he stay upstairs alone so he could ransack the others' rooms for valuables? Could it be Cherise? Had she stolen her own necklace and then returned it to herself just to throw Liz off the scent? And what about Penny? Had she even brought jewelry from home? Was that why she hadn't wanted the police called? And the money envelope had never turned up, and Vivian *had* been alone in the kitchen on Friday before it disappeared.

Shivering, Liz stepped inside the utility room after pushing Beans's heavy weight away from the door. She shook her head as she pulled off her boots. Beans hadn't even twitched. *If only I could sleep so deeply.* Reaching for her shoes, she nearly jumped out of her skin at the "hello!" right behind her.

"Goodness, Cherise." Liz took a deep breath and hung up her down-filled parka.

"My so-called partner, Paul, won't come out of his room again." She stamped one dainty foot. "We should study our list of clues and narrow down the suspects so we can be ready for Act Five and piece it all together."

"I agree." Liz led the way to the kitchen. "Let me think." She poured them both a cup of coffee. "Maybe he's indisposed. It's possible that my meat pudding didn't sit too well with him this morning."

Cherise snorted. "Ha. If his stomach hurts, it's because he stuffs himself beyond capacity at every turn."

As innkeeper, it was her job to make guests comfortable, not judge them. "A young woman who works for me during the week, Sarah Borkholder, always recommends a home remedy with apple cider vinegar. She says it can immediately settle a stomach. Let me offer that to him and see if it helps."

After mixing two tablespoons of apple cider vinegar into a small glass of apple juice, Liz carried the glass upstairs. At the second-floor landing, she paused in surprise. Peering through the keyhole into the Amish Room was Vivian. As she reached to turn the doorknob, Liz cleared her throat.

Vivian whipped around, her face flushed bright pink. Without a word, she scooted across the landing and disappeared into the Heirloom Room.

Liz shook her head. What was that all about? Was Vivian spying on Jeremy, or was she merely hoping to get a glimpse of his reality TV script? Or—good heavens—was Vivian the elusive person who'd been sneaking into other guests' rooms to take things? Liz mentally shook herself. *One thing at a time.* First she had to budge Paul out of his room before Cherise had a full-blown conniption.

Liz stepped over to the Somewhere in Time Room and knocked. Paul didn't answer, nor did she hear any movement inside. She knocked louder and waited. She hated to wake him up if he was sleeping, but it was early in the day for a nap.

"Paul?" she called.

When there was still no answer, Liz decided she'd better peek in. Perhaps he'd snuck out to the bakery next door for some extra pastries—she now recalled seeing him in the foyer earlier—but she thought it was wise to check and make sure he was all right.

She opened the door and stuck her head in. "Paul? It's Liz. Are you all right?" The bed was rumpled, but empty. The door to the bathroom was open, and it was dark in there. Well, she'd just leave the apple cider vinegar drink on his desk with a note. She needed to finish a few things downstairs before the final act at eleven o'clock.

On his desk was an open laptop instead of the previous scribbled papers and notes. Had he typed up his clues? If that was the case, he was certainly taking the mystery weekend more seriously than she'd thought.

She moved the laptop over a couple inches to make room for the juice. Glancing down, she caught a headline on the open document: *Give This B&B a Pass!* Confused, but curious, she wondered what he'd been researching on the Internet. Was he moving on to other bed-and-breakfast places after leaving hers?

But then her eye zeroed in on two things in the opening paragraph: her own name, and the name Olde Mansion Inn.

Stunned, Liz read the full first paragraph. Surely she was mistaken about what she was reading.

She leaned over to scan the screen, not even caring now how snoopy she was being. She read aloud the scathing review of the mystery weekend, her voice a raspy whisper. The terrible truth finally dawned on her. She scrolled to the end of the article, hoping against hope that she was wrong.

But no. There was his name.

Drew Garrett.

Her face flushed hot, while her fingers were clammy. This overweight frumpy guest wasn't a reclusive, shy retiree named Paul Levine. The man who'd written the scathing criticism of her inn was the reviewer she hadn't been expecting until the following day.

He'd come incognito, posing as a mystery weekend guest, but was really there to evaluate her inn. Liz went back to the beginning and skimmed the whole article, feeling sicker by the moment. Her knees quivered, and she collapsed onto the desk chair. He'd written how he'd expected an Amish experience since the inn was in Amish country—pumpkin bread and zucchini bread, fresh eggs, and apple butter right off the farm. He described instead the "inedible Victorian London dishes" he was served. No mention was made that he'd signed up for a Sherlock mystery weekend.

Judging from the name of the file, this was his review for the travel magazine scheduled for publication in January. She'd never felt so demoralized.

Liz tried to breathe deeply, but her throat felt constricted, as if it were being squeezed in a vise. This travel magazine review would do her business untold damage. And she didn't have to be told that the Olde Mansion Inn wouldn't be featured in his upcoming book on recommended B&Bs either.

Still dazed, she left his room, closing the door behind her, and descended the staircase on shaky legs. She kept a firm grip on the banister.

No matter how the mystery weekend finished for the guests, it was already a massive failure for Liz.

By ten forty, all the actors had arrived dressed in their costumes. Liz greeted everyone, but her mind was only half aware of her surroundings. *Focus!* she told herself sternly. *You still have a job to do.* While the actors chatted, Liz motioned for David to come aside.

She led him to the kitchen, then turned to face him. "I have a quick question for you."

"Sure." He leaned against the counter, his tall frame towering over her.

Glancing over her shoulder, Liz lowered her voice in case anyone waltzed in unannounced. "One of our guests, the movie actress, voiced a concern this morning. She wondered why you were up on the third floor yesterday." She waited, but he was silent. "She saw you coming down the stairs," she added, suddenly realizing how accusatory that sounded. "You have to understand. With the unexplained thefts, guests are a bit nervous."

"I wasn't on the third floor." David crossed his lean arms over his narrow chest. "Not yesterday, not ever."

Liz wished with all her heart she could drop it, but after observing his odd behavior when following the Amish woman and later at the lake, she couldn't let this go unresolved. Her gut told her that Cherise was telling the truth about what she'd seen.

"Please think back," Liz said firmly. "Maybe you forgot why you were upstairs."

David set his jaw and stared at the floor. He uncrossed his arms, then crossed them again. Voices floated in, sounding as if both actors and guests were geared up to have a good time in the final hours of the mystery weekend.

"David?" she prodded.

He stood to his full height and dropped his arms to his sides. "Yes, I was up on the third floor briefly, but I didn't do anything wrong."

"I had assured the guests that no one but them would be allowed on the second and third floors. So I need to know why you were there."

"I was looking out the window."

"Overlooking the lake?" she asked, recalling his rendezvous at Jaynes Lake.

"No, the window on the other side, overlooking the town square." He sounded defiant now. "The view is better there than from a ground floor window."

"You climbed to the third floor to look out a window? That's all?"

"That's all." David stretched to his full height. "I could pass a lie detector test about it."

Liz smiled then. "That isn't necessary. Were you looking for anything in particular?"

She detected a slight hesitation before he shook his head, and she didn't like it. *What is he hiding? And does it have any bearing on the thefts this weekend?*

"Okay," she finally said, glancing at her watch. "I need to change and make sure the dining room is all set for Act Five. You ready for the grand finale?"

"I think so." He headed to the rotunda, then stopped in the kitchen doorway and turned back. "I really only went upstairs to look out the window. I'm sorry if I scared someone."

Liz nodded and wished she believed him wholeheartedly. But there was no time to talk further, and she sensed that he'd given her all the information he intended to reveal. She ran to put on her Victorian outfit. Five minutes later, she was ushering the guests into the dining room for Act Five. She deliberately avoided making eye contact with "Paul" as she gave the introduction.

"Act Five takes place the following morning in the Braithwaite home. James and Nettie Braithwaite are at breakfast. The morning's newspaper is folded and waiting on the table. This is the final act. Any remaining clues needed to solve the crime will be found in Act Five."

She stepped back near the door and motioned for Doyle, the butler, to enter the dining room and begin.

DOYLE (carrying the morning newspaper and acting irritated): That new maid is slipshod, sir. (He takes the paper on the table and throws it in a wastebasket.)

NETTIE BRAITHWAITE: Slipshod, Doyle?

DOYLE: I told her to throw yesterday's paper in the bin. This was just delivered, sir. (He leaves the newspaper beside Braithwaite's plate and retires.)

NETTIE (watching her husband scan the front page): Is there anything of significance in the paper this morning?

JAMES BRAITHWAITE (laughs): Here's something spot on from an article called 'Advice to wives.' Do listen. 'The wife's motto must be never to irritate her husband and never, if possible, to make scenes.' Very wise advice, my dear.

NETTIE: When have you ever known me to make a scene? (She leans over to read.) Let me see what else it says. Hmmm. 'If irritation should occur, a woman must expect to hear from most men a strength and vehemence of language far more than the occasion requires.' (She nods and hides a smile behind her napkin.) That is certainly true.

JAMES (harrumphs and shakes the paper, turns a page,

and scans the headlines): Here's 'Advice to a Young Lawyer.'
Ridiculous counsel. (Reads more silently.) Ho, what's this?
(His eyes widen.) No! (He clutches his chest, gasps, and falls
to the floor.)

NETTIE (screaming): Doyle, get the doctor!

Doyle runs out, then returns with Dr. Fitzhugh.

DR. FITZHUGH (listens to James's heart, then his
breathing): I'm sorry, Mrs. Braithwaite. He's gone.

NETTIE (weeping while lying on James' chest): James!
James!

Liz stepped forward. "This ends Act Five. That's the final scene and final clue. As before, you have five minutes to note anything of significance, in particular critical clues. At the end of five minutes, I will give you instructions for presenting your solutions later."

The actors remained frozen in place while the six costumed guests moved forward. As usual, Jeremy and Vivian forged ahead to obtain the first up-close look at the scene. Cherise whipped out her smartphone and snapped picture after picture. Penny and Louise huddled together, whispering.

Liz continued to avoid looking at Paul—or Drew—while she counted the minutes.

"Five minutes are up." Liz motioned for the guests to gather in the rotunda. She stood on the bottom step of the staircase to give her instructions. "Please reconvene in the sitting room at one o'clock this afternoon with your answers to the mystery. At that time, the solution will be revealed." She raised her voice to make sure even Louise heard the directions. "Each Sherlock/Watson pair must bring with them, *in writing*, the answers to four questions. You'll want to write these questions down. First, who stole the rare Dickens edition? Second, who killed James Braithwaite? Third, how was he killed? And fourth, what was the killer's motive? After you've written down your answers to these questions, be sure to sign your papers."

Liz supposed, for Cherise's sake, she ought to remind Paul to spend some time talking with his teammate about solving the crime. She just couldn't carry on with the charade, though, not now that she knew who he *really* was.

Silently she apologized to Cherise, but the movie starlet was on her own. Liz had enough unsolved problems of her own to deal with.

14

After writing down Liz's instructions, the guests split up and headed off to compare their clues and notes. Liz was gratified to hear the various animated comments. Two teams were convinced that they'd figured out the answer to the crime. There was much whispering as they searched out private spots where they could put their heads together.

Liz turned back to the dining room, where Bert, Naomi, and David were laughing about Jackson's theatrical collapse at the end of Act Five.

"It was bad enough that I hit the back of my head on the floor," he said, "but then Naomi fell on my chest so hard that I knew she'd cracked one of my ribs."

"Oh, poor thing," Naomi said, her chuckle at odds with her words.

Liz hung back and listened for a moment, grateful that they'd had a good time.

Moving through the group with a big smile, Liz thanked Bert again for his convincing performance as the butler. Out of the corner of her eye, Liz noticed David pull a note from the pocket of his doctor's coat. When he read it, a troubled expression fleetingly crossed his face before he shoved it back in his pocket. Although curious, Liz wasn't in the mood to ask him any more personal questions.

Instead, she chatted with the others as she returned the dining room to its natural state. She boxed up the props to return to the playhouse when she took back the costumes she'd borrowed. She'd keep the "London" newspapers as souvenirs, since she'd gotten them online. One paper was on the floor, crumpled, where James Braithwaite had fallen with it clutched in his hand. She found the other paper in the wastebasket that had gotten shoved behind the burgundy wingback chair. She snuffed out the candles in both candelabra, waving her hand to dissipate the swirls of smoke.

Liz grabbed two free minutes with Naomi after the room cleared, but there wasn't time to do anything but give her a quick recap of how things were going. "Every time I figure out one thing, two other mysterious things happen," Liz said. "And just about the time I think I really should call in the police, something is proved to be a prank. I don't want to waste their time, but something wrong is going on here. I'm determined to find out what it is."

"Please don't do anything dangerous," Naomi said. "Promise me."

"I promise." *I won't do anything dangerous on purpose, anyway.*

Liz decided to remain in costume herself until after the villain had been revealed and her guests departed after lunch. Making a quick sweep through the downstairs rooms to pick up any trash and straighten cushions and magazines, she found the library occupied by Jeremy and Vivian. Earlier Penny and Louise had laid claim to the four-season room. She suspected that Paul had disappeared upstairs to finish his malicious review and character assassination. In case Cherise waited to ambush her in the kitchen again, Liz detoured into the empty sitting room.

Only it wasn't empty. David stood by the fireplace, slumped against it with one arm on the mantel, a perfect picture of defeat. In his shaking hand, he held the note she'd glimpsed earlier. At least, it looked the same, a note written on one of the Sherlock Holmes notepads she'd given each guest with the Sherlock stamp at the top. Liz cleared her throat, and David whipped around.

"Are you all right?" she asked.

Almost reflexively, David concealed the note behind him. He

glanced at her but didn't meet her eye. "Yes, but I need to get home and change, then get to the hospital for my shift."

"Okay. Please bring your costume back to me tomorrow, if you can, so I can turn it in."

David nodded, then tossed the note into the low-burning flames. It caught fire immediately. He stepped around her and left.

The second the door closed, Liz rushed to the fireplace. Using the sharp poker, she stabbed the note and pulled it from the fire. After she blew out the flame, little was left.

She was careful not to touch the burned edges as she turned the tiny remaining piece over. The few words left were severely scorched. She frowned and stared, unable to take it in at first. But no, it wasn't her imagination. Two words were clearly legible: *murderer* and *magic*.

The half-burned, but telltale Sherlock symbol stamped on the top of the note showed that the paper had come from one of the guests' notepads. Was it someone's list of clues? Or was the note exactly what it sounded like: a threat?

Liz closed her eyes and recalled the scene in the dining room when the acting was over and the guests moved in closer to examine the clues. David had been kneeling on the floor, next to Jackson's "dead" body. Any of the guests could have come from behind, brushed against David, stuck the note into his pocket, and moved on past. A reverse pickpocketing, so to speak.

While people in town might know he was an amateur magician, how would the guests know? Could the note have come from one of the actors? And *murderer*? Liz couldn't ignore the fact that David had been caught where he shouldn't be, and he'd been very reluctant to answer questions about it. The reason he finally gave was iffy at best.

Before Liz could discover where David had disappeared to, she heard the remaining actors gather in the rotunda. Sliding the burned scrap of paper into a book, she placed it on the shelf to deal with later. She felt she owed it to David to ask him about the note before she mentioned it to anyone else.

She hurried out to see her friends off. If possible, she hoped to ask Jackson for some advice about her spiteful undercover reviewer. Maybe there was some chance—although she couldn't imagine what—that her inn's good name could still be salvaged.

"There you are," Naomi called when Liz stepped into the foyer. "We're off now, but I promise to turn in my costume at the playhouse tomorrow."

"Thanks. If they decide there's a cleaning fee, remind them that the bill comes to me."

Naomi laughed and brushed at her long skirt. "I suppose throwing myself on the floor today didn't help."

Liz hugged her friend. "It was worth any cleaning fee I might need to pay."

Bert nodded stiffly, as if still playing the butler. "I barely bent from the waist at any time. I doubt there's even a wrinkle in my costume." With a wave, he stepped out into the foyer, pulled the collar of his coat up around his face, and left.

"I'm off too," Naomi said. "I'll be at the bakery for a while if you need anything."

Jackson started after her, but Liz laid a hand on his arm. "Do you have a minute?"

"Sure." He grinned at her, then studied her closely, and his smile disappeared. "What's wrong?"

"You won't believe it." Liz nodded toward the kitchen. "I need some advice from a good businessman."

Jackson perched on one of the kitchen stools at the island counter. "Coffee?" Liz asked. "Or some coffee cake?"

"Or both?"

"Both it is."

While Jackson ate, Liz sat where she could see into the rotunda. She didn't want anyone walking in unannounced. When she revealed what she'd learned, that Paul Levine was really Drew Garrett and he'd come incognito for the weekend, Jackson stopped chewing and lowered his fork to his plate. He gave Liz his undivided attention, and she appreciated it.

"And you expected him to arrive tomorrow instead?"

"Yes, that's when he has a reservation. He wanted to stay in the Amish Room and have authentic Amish dishes, which I planned for tomorrow. Instead, it's been a zoo this weekend for various reasons, he was served Victorian food he didn't like, and he's staying in the Somewhere in Time Room, which isn't the least bit Amish. Not only does his review for the travel magazine trash my inn, but after he drops his bombshell, there won't be a chance I'll be included in his book on the best B&Bs in the country." She slumped at the counter, her chin in her cupped palm. "This is the most humiliating thing I've ever had happen, and the review isn't even published yet."

"Maybe no one will actually read the review."

"The print magazine has an online edition too." Liz closed her eyes as she imagined the impact. "It only takes a few people reposting the review for something to go viral." She gripped her fingers together, shocked at the realization that if Drew walked in at that moment, she could cheerfully choke him.

"You have every right to feel angry, Liz. This was an underhanded thing to do."

"My feelings are a real jumble right now. How could he be so sneaky, lying to me about who he is and why he's here? At least I understand now why he was being such a hermit."

"You want advice, you said?" Jackson ate the last of his coffee cake.

"Yes, I need every pearl of wisdom you can spare."

"Okay. If it had happened to me, I would confront him with what you know before he leaves today. Even though he must realize this, I'd explain that this wasn't a normal weekend at the inn."

Liz bit the inside of her cheek. "If I do that though," she said, "he might make the review even worse. He could truthfully say that I was poking and prying in his room, which should have been private. A review that says the guests have no privacy would mean the end of my business."

"It's entirely up to you." Jackson drained his coffee cup. "I just hate to see him get away with what he's done. If you left the glass of juice beside his computer, won't he already suspect that you saw and read the review?"

"That's true."

"Then what do you have to lose?"

Liz prayed quietly for direction. She knew she was in the wrong for reading the article without permission. But Jackson was right. Drew had been dishonest, and *she* was the one who would pay heavily for *his* actions. That was wrong, no matter what she'd done.

She slid down from her stool. "I'll talk to him right now. I don't want to miss him in case he sneaks out early." She squeezed Jackson's arm. "Thank you."

As she mounted the staircase, one hand holding up her long skirt and her other hand gripping the banister, she trembled at the imminent confrontation. No matter what he accused her of in return, bringing the man's deception out in the open felt like the right thing to do. If only she was half as bold as Jackson seemed to think she was. She told herself that fear didn't have to stop her, that whatever scary thing needed to be done, she could do it.

Liz allowed herself a moment for her heart to slow down before knocking on the door of the Somewhere in Time Room. When the reviewer answered the door, Liz asked him first if he'd found her note and the apple cider vinegar she'd left for him.

"Yes. Thank you." His lips smiled, but his eyes had a wary—even distrustful—expression.

"Could I come in for a moment?"

He hesitated. "Is this about spending more time with that airhead?"

Liz bristled at his description of Cherise. "No, it isn't," she said, "but it's a discussion you might prefer *not* to have out here in the hallway."

He studied her a moment, eyes squinted with suspicion, then stepped back and opened the door wide. After she came in, he closed the door and moved several feet away. Liz leaned back against the door and gripped the knob behind her back.

"As you may have guessed," Liz said, "I saw your review when I left the apple juice on your desk. I wasn't expecting you, *Mr. Garrett*, until tomorrow, the day of your reservation. And naturally I expected you under your real name."

He raised one eyebrow, giving his pudgy face an arrogance that made Liz's palm itch. "I find, Ms. Eckardt, that I always have a more honest experience of a B&B when I show up unexpectedly."

"But in this case, it wasn't a typical experience, was it?" When he didn't answer, she added, "You knew this was a mystery weekend, where you would interact with other guests, and a weekend in which I specifically said I would serve Victorian food. The confirmation letter you mailed back indicated that you were fine with that."

"I thought it would taste better."

Liz stared at the insolent man. Apparently he saw nothing wrong with what he'd done. She doubted that arguing would get her anywhere either. Should she simply exit quietly, dignity intact, and accept defeat?

She turned to leave, but paused with her hand on the doorknob. "You said you usually had a more honest experience this way, and it's true that you received no special treatment, no catering to you in return for a rave review. I treat all my guests the same. However, when you have to be *dis*honest to meet your objective, there's something wrong with your methods."

She opened the door and stepped into the central hall. Ignoring Vivian, who was peeping at her from the slightly ajar door of the Heirloom Room, Liz swept across the landing, head held high. Keeping her back straight, feeling regal in her royal blue skirt, she'd glided down a dozen steps when she heard her name called.

"Ms. Eckardt? Wait a moment."

Liz paused and looked up. Drew Garrett stood at the top of the stairs. "I will *try* to return for a normal weekend to get a better sample of your Amish experience."

Liz leaned her head to one side. "You wouldn't want to simply stay another night, let me clean the Amish Room, and move in there tomorrow, as planned?"

"No. I have another commitment."

"Had you planned to tell me, or were you going to simply not show up tomorrow?"

He hesitated. "I was going to leave a note in my room." He cleared his throat. "But as I said, I will try to return for an authentic Amish weekend."

"Thank you. I would appreciate that."

"Let me be clear. I'm *not* promising a good review, or that I'll come back before my book deadline."

Liz nodded. "I understand." While she hated to lose the opportunity for nationwide advertising in his book, Liz felt she'd now settle happily for no review at all from him, anywhere.

Downstairs, as she passed the sitting room, Liz remembered the half-burned menacing note David had received. It must have come from one of the guests since it was written on the Sherlock Holmes notepads.

Magic? Murderer? What in the world was going on? The first chance she had, she'd track David down and ask him.

He was an enigma, and she wasn't sure what to do. He'd lived in Pleasant Creek such a short time. No one—including Liz—knew much about him. He hadn't wanted to talk about the note, but Liz felt responsible. He'd been at the inn doing her a big favor, and she hated to think one of her guests might have threatened him.

Something she'd caught in David's expression when he'd first read the note made her suspect that he knew what the accuser meant. He hadn't appeared puzzled by the note or even shocked. He'd looked frightened, as if his secret had been found out. If he weren't guilty of anything, surely he would have shown her the note instead of throwing it into the fire to be destroyed.

What more could go wrong in a simple mystery game weekend?

By the time she entered the kitchen, Jackson was rinsing his plate and cup at the sink.

"You don't have to do that," Liz said, although she had to admit he looked awfully nice standing there in her kitchen at the sink. Like he belonged there.

"I have to go actually, but I wanted to wait and hear how your talk went. Did you see him?" He pointed toward the ceiling.

"Yes, and I'm glad I took your advice. He didn't apologize or anything, but he said he would try to come back and stay another weekend before his book deadline, so there's still a small chance I'll make it into the book."

"And the rotten review he wrote?"

Liz thought back. "Well, he agreed with me that he'd been unfair, but he didn't specifically say that he wouldn't publish the review." She rubbed the back of her neck. "Time will tell, I guess."

"It may still turn out well for you."

"I hope so."

She stood in the doorway and waved when he drove off, then hurried back inside. Despite the midday sun directly overhead, it couldn't be more than thirty degrees outside. And that was without figuring in the wind chill.

Pouring a mug of coffee for herself, Liz carried it into her private quarters. With her laptop open on her bed, she plumped up the pillows at the headboard and leaned back. While the guests were off studying their clues, she wanted to do some sleuthing of her own.

But where to start? She finally chose to do Internet searches using different combinations of the words *David Mills*, *murderer*, and *magic*. A whole array of articles came up, many about murder mysteries written by someone of that name, but the photo of the author clearly wasn't her friend, David.

Liz eased back on her pillows, wondering how to refine the search. She tried other combinations, including *magician* instead of *magic*. One story popped up several times, complete with multiple color photos. The article, called "Death by Magic", was about a man named David *Miller*, not Mills. Liz leaned closer to her screen to scrutinize the photo dated fifteen years ago.

Her eyes weren't deceiving her. It was definitely a picture of David Mills. In the photos, he was onstage, dressed in a flowing red cape and billed as "The Great Shima." Scanning the first article, she discovered that the photo had been taken at a national CEO conference in California where David had been the featured entertainment.

He's much more than an amateur magician, the article claimed. Liz continued to read. David had been a professional performer working at a very fancy venue. Why had he downplayed his talents so much? And why had he left a professional career as an entertainer to work in the cafeteria of a small Midwestern hospital?

She kept reading, scrolling down past many photos taken during his various acts. They ranged from making audience members disappear and transforming a bucket of water into a bucket of cash to levitating himself and swallowing fire. And then she found it.

"Oh, no," she murmured. "How awful."

The article described how a volunteer from the audience had died onstage during one of the magician's tricks called a "water barrel escape." David had been placed in a water barrel; then it was filled with water by an audience member and sealed. The trick was to get out before he drowned.

While he'd worked to escape, pounding on the barrel for dramatic effect, the volunteer from the audience had panicked, believing Miller was truly drowning. While Miller successfully escaped from the water-filled barrel, the audience volunteer had died of a heart attack onstage. At the time the article was written, the name of the victim hadn't been released, pending notification of next of kin.

David Mills, cafeteria worker, had definitely been David Miller, The Great Shima. Had he left the entertainment field and changed his name because he was traumatized by what had happened? Or had he wanted to escape a scandal?

When she heard the front door open and voices echoing in the rotunda, she realized with a start that it was nearly one o'clock—time to unveil the answer to the mystery weekend. She'd have to search for more articles later and hunt for more details. Or maybe she would simply ask David when he returned his costume to her.

But when she went to the dining room to clean up any spills or dirty dishes, she found his costume on the sideboard. Neatly folded, it had a note on top.

Thank you for asking me to participate this weekend, Liz. I enjoyed it very much.

So he isn't coming back. David had left his costume, but he'd taken a load of unanswered questions with him.

15

When the Sherlocks and Watsons gathered for the unveiling of the mystery's solution, Liz approached their final time together with determined enthusiasm. She was adamant that she would stay in control of the situation and end this chaotic weekend on a high note. Then she would send them on their way with a smile. And then collapse.

They met in the library, and the glowing coals in the fireplace produced enough heat to make it cozy. Liz had lined up the prizes she'd purchased on a bookshelf. There were several Sherlock puzzle books, a mug with his silhouette painted on it, a bust of his head and shoulders, and a Sherlock nutcracker. She would make sure each guest who wanted a memento of the weekend received a prize. But first choice would go the winning team, if there was one.

Liz handed out three envelopes. "Each team should have already written the answers to the questions I gave you earlier on a sheet of paper. Please put your answers in these envelopes and hand them back to me."

She waited until each team complied and handed her their responses.

"Thank you," Liz said. "First I'll reveal the solution. Then we'll see if anyone—or everyone—guessed correctly." She laughed. "Then again, Sherlock never guessed. He *knew*."

Liz scanned the group of six sleuths. How differently she perceived them now compared to when they'd arrived on Friday and met in the library. All of them except Paul—Drew—looked eager to hear the answer. The reviewer hung back, obviously bored and begrudging his time.

"I feel like we need a drumroll," Liz said, opening her folded paper. "Here are the answers to the questions I posed to you earlier today. Jeremy, I'm going to ask for no discussion of the answers until I reveal all four parts of the solution, okay?" She cleared her throat. "First, who stole the rare edition? The villain is Mr. Braithwaite's friend, the newspaper publisher, Godfrey Denshaw. He stole the rare Dickens book in the first place, a book he had wanted for a long time. We learned in Act One that the publisher friend had seen the rare book before he or his reporter wrote an article announcing its purchase. Later, the newspaper article reporting the offered reward proved that someone at the newspaper office had seen the stolen book in person. It described details the owner didn't reveal to the police."

Liz could tell already that one pair of detectives was out of the running. Cherise was literally pouting. Even her bouncy hair drooped.

"Second, who killed James Braithwaite?" Liz scanned the group. "Also his friend, the newspaper publisher, Godfrey Denshaw."

"What?" Louise demanded. "That can't be right."

Liz smiled. "Third, what was the weapon used to kill him?" She looked around, drawing out the moment. "A newspaper article."

"He was killed with a piece of paper?" Penny exclaimed.

"No, not with the newspaper itself," Liz explained, "but an article on the front page of the paper he read at breakfast." She held up the newspaper in question and pointed to an article near the bottom of the front page. "Vivian, could you read this, please?"

"Sure." She cleared her throat. "'Ocean Liner Capsizes. All On Board Lost' is the title," she said. "The article says, 'Late Friday night an ocean liner, the *Indian Queen*, was caught in a severe storm off the coast of Morocco and capsized in heavy seas. All 178 passengers and twelve crew members went down with the ship. No survivors have been found. Names are being withheld pending notification of next of kin.'"

"Thank you, Vivian," Liz said. "This is the weapon created by the publisher. He heard from Braithwaite in Act Four that his son was sailing home on that ship the next day. So, he stayed late in the newspaper office that night and created a different front page of the next morning's newspaper. He delivered it himself and left it on the porch early the next morning. If you had examined both newspapers—the one in the wastebasket that the butler threw away and the one on the table—you would have noticed that both had the *same date* and nearly all the *same articles*. The only difference was that the second newspaper had deleted one article and replaced it with the phony article about the drownings."

Questions and comments erupted, but Liz held up her hand.

"Let me finish before we discuss the clues," she said. "The maid wasn't derelict in her duties at all. The butler didn't realize that the newspaper he discovered on the veranda was the *second* newspaper delivered that morning. It included the fictitious account of Mr. Braithwaite's son's death. The publisher friend, knowing about the son's arrival and Braithwaite's weak heart, along with his propensity to get overexcited, hoped that the article would bring on a collapse. And it did."

Penny frowned. "I have a question about that."

Liz held up her sheet of answers. "If you could hold your question for just a minute, I'll reveal the motives first."

"Okay."

"The fourth question was about motive," Liz said. "We have two crimes, but for a correct answer, you only had to give one motive." She cleared her throat. "The motive for the murder was simply to cover up the original burglary. The burglary of the Dickens book was motivated by greed, as the newspaper publisher wanted that rare special edition for his own collection. Remember, in Act One, James Braithwaite mentions that his publishing friend had written the article about the Dickens book after James showed it to him."

Jeremy and Vivian leaned forward on the couch now, their animated faces barely concealing their jubilation.

Liz held up the three colored envelopes and opened the first one, signed *The Rollinses*. They had deduced that the butler was the thief, and the motive for stealing the valuable book was greed because he wanted to set up his own shop somewhere with the proceeds from selling it. And no weapon had been needed—he had simply stolen the book when he was in the room alone with it. The Rollinses guessed that Doyle had killed Mr. Braithwaite by poisoning his food.

"Those are good logical conclusions," Liz said, "but not the winning answers, I'm afraid."

Penny pushed forward. "May I ask my question now?"

"Let me read the other answers first. If someone got it right, I'll let them explain how they reached their conclusions." She glanced at the other two teams.

The reviewer stared out the window and didn't appear to be listening. Cherise was scrolling through the photos on her phone and frowning. Vivian and Jeremy wore matching expressions of glee.

Liz opened the second envelope, and the sheet was signed only by Cherise. Her answer, written in large loopy letters, said Nettie Braithwaite had stolen the rare edition, and her motive was to get her husband's attention away from his musty books. She was sure James Braithwaite's anger had brought on the heart attack that killed him. Nettie Braithwaite's weapon had been a woman's "naturally superior cunning."

"Even though this isn't the winning answer, and Nettie's ploy to get more attention backfired in the end," Liz said, grinning, "I like it."

Cherise nodded, the set of her lips grim. "When you're done, I have something to show you."

"Certainly." Liz reached for the last envelope. "Now, let's see if our last team solved it."

By the way Vivian tapped her feet, and from Jeremy's smug look, she guessed they'd cracked it. She opened the last envelope and read, "The newspaper publisher is the villain. He stole the book and also caused Braithwaite's death by heart attack. The weapon he used was the false report he published about the Braithwaites' son's ship going down. His motive for stealing the book was greed, and the motive for the murder was to hide the theft."

Liz waved their sheet of answers. "Well done." She passed around the paper so all the guests could see what they'd written. "Congratulations to you both. Choose your prizes." She motioned toward the shelf behind her. "You worked well together."

Cherise stepped forward then. "No, you *cheated* well together."

Vivian's mouth dropped open. "What? We did not."

Jeremy's scowl was threatening. "You had access to the same clues we did. We can't help it if you didn't look closely."

Liz stepped in then. "Jeremy's right, Cherise. You all got the same five minutes to examine the evidence for each act before I cleaned it away."

Cherise waved her smartphone. "A picture is worth a thousand words. You learn that as an actress."

Jeremy sneered. "So?"

"So, I took dozens of photos of the crime scenes so I didn't have to rely on my memory." She motioned for the Rollins ladies to come closer so they could also see. "Look at my photos of Act Five." She showed Liz and the Rollins ladies each picture, frame by frame.

Liz squinted as she studied each photo. "I'm afraid I don't see what you're hinting at."

"Look again. There's a reason that the rest of us couldn't compare the two newspapers. See? In the photo taken right after Braithwaite was pronounced dead, there's the wastebasket with the first newspaper sticking out of it. It's right by the wingback chair that's in the corner."

"So?" Jeremy demanded.

"So, look at this photo taken later at the same angle. Braithwaite is still lying there, and the chair is in the picture, but there's no wastebasket."

"That *is* puzzling," Liz admitted. Then a memory jolted her from when she'd straightened the dining room. She'd found the wastebasket *behind* the burgundy wingback chair.

"How did it move?" Louise asked, peering at the tiny camera images.

"It didn't move, at least, not by itself," Cherise said. "It was *helped* out of sight before the rest of us could see it."

Vivian puffed up like a cobra. "Are you accusing me?"

"No," Cherise said calmly, "I'll let the photo do that. As I said, a picture's worth a thousand words."

Cherise turned in a slow circle so each person in the room could see the photo. It was a close-up of James Braithwaite on the floor, but the background showed the lower part of someone's leg in brown trousers. Brown equaled a Watson costume. "Note the shoe," Cherise said. Peeping out beneath the baggy trouser leg was a black ballet flat. And the foot appeared to be nudging the wastebasket around the wingback chair where it would be out of sight.

Appalled, Liz glanced at Vivian, hoping her face didn't mirror the disgust she felt. The picture couldn't lie. Vivian had worn those particular ballet flats all weekend.

"No wonder you got all the answers right," Louise said.

Penny stood with hands on hips. "We could have figured it out too, if we'd had all the facts."

Jeremy snorted. "It wouldn't have mattered."

Liz wanted to knock the winning team's heads together. "Obviously, Jeremy and Vivian are disqualified. You others may choose a prize here on the shelf as a—" She'd started to say "as a happy reminder of the weekend," but she doubted if their memories were any better than hers. "As a reminder to keep reading Sherlock Holmes stories," she finished lamely.

How could she possibly salvage a positive ending now? Liz had no idea, so she simply reminded them that checkout was between two and three o'clock that afternoon and to drive safely getting home.

She also reminded herself never to run another mystery weekend. Her shoulders sagged. Not ever again.

As the guests dispersed, Liz suddenly remembered her last duty as hostess.

"Wait!" she called. "One of the fun things for the Victorian weekend was our pickpocket working in the dark London streets as you moved about the lower level. The items have been in my safe this weekend." She reached for the small items she'd stashed a little while ago behind an Indiana travel guide on the library shelf. "I have three things to return. Here's a beautiful lace handkerchief belonging to Louise. And here's a lovely watch." She handed it to a crestfallen Vivian who refused to meet her eye. "And here's Jeremy's—"

"I'll take that," he interrupted, grabbing the rabbit's foot.

Liz reminded them all to leave the Holmes and Watson costumes in their rooms.

Wearily, Liz counted the minutes until the last person should be checked out and peace would descend on the inn. It couldn't come too soon for her. The last forty-eight hours had felt like a month.

But harmony didn't even last until the guests reached the top of the staircase.

"Hey," Jeremy shouted. "I never got my gold antique coin back."

Liz froze. What gold antique coin? That good luck piece he'd mentioned a couple times that weekend?

Vivian's voice was conciliatory. "It's small. Liz probably just overlooked it in the safe."

"Or she intends to keep it," he retorted.

Liz clenched her fists until her nails dug into her palms. *How dare he?*

"Well, if she doesn't have it," Jeremy said, "one of you others stole it!"

This was worse than hosting a group of bratty children.

Wearily Liz climbed the staircase. "Can I help, Jeremy?" she called as she neared the second floor.

Jeremy met her on the stairs. "Did your pickpocket turn in an antique gold coin? I always carry it. I just noticed it was missing."

"I've seen it," Vivian called over the banister. "He always has it."

"Well, we know how truthful *you* are," Penny snapped.

Vivian flushed and disappeared.

Liz climbed the rest of the way to the second floor. "No, I didn't have a gold coin in my safe. Nothing like that was turned in."

Cherise spoke up then. "I saw the gold coin when he passed it around during breakfast yesterday."

"There, see? Maybe your pickpocket kept it."

Liz shook her head, but she couldn't help remembering how David had left the moment Act Five was over around noon. *Had* he pickpocketed the coin, believing it was valuable, and escaped with it?

"Either way," Jeremy said, "you're responsible."

Liz sneaked a quick look at Louise. Could she have taken it and then forgotten about it? But no, not if he had it in his pocket. Even if Louise was adept at sleight of hand, she couldn't move quickly enough to get away with it.

Louise leaned close to her daughter, but her stage whisper carried clearly. "You promised this mystery weekend would be fun, not someplace with a real criminal on the loose. I was afraid to stay alone in my room."

"I'm sorry, Mother. I'll make it up to you."

"I just had heart surgery," Louise reminded her.

"I know." Penny wrapped an arm around her mother's shoulders. "I hope you haven't been traumatized."

I sincerely hope not too. Liz watched them head up to the third floor as visions of being sued danced in her head.

"Look," Jeremy said, "what are you going to do about my missing coin? I know its worth. It was appraised last year for $3,500!"

"Oh, come on," Cherise said with a snort.

"It's true!" Jeremy snapped. "I'm calling my lawyer right now to have him email me a copy of the appraiser's estimate."

Liz gazed from one guest to another, studying each one in turn. She wondered if, as owner of the inn, she could still run away from home.

16

"We'll get to the bottom of this," Liz assured Jeremy, although she had no idea how. But given the worth of the stolen item this time, she had no choice but to report it. "All of you, please change out of your costumes and pack up, but don't leave yet."

Ignoring the groans and Cherise's insistent protest about being treated like a criminal, Liz summoned every last vestige of dignity and charm, then glided down the stairs in her lovely Victorian-era dress. Staying in the rotunda to make sure no one left, she called Stan Houghton, Pleasant Creek's police chief.

"Chief, I'm sorry to bother you on a Sunday afternoon," she said. "Did I interrupt your afternoon nap?"

Houghton chuckled. "I wish. What can I do for you today?"

Liz gave a short summary of the things that had gone missing that weekend, but were then returned, including the items pickpocketed on purpose. "I didn't report the things that were returned," she said, "but a guest just now revealed that his gold coin worth $3,500 is missing."

"From his pocket?"

"That's what he claims."

"Did your pickpocket take it?"

"I don't think so, but I don't know for sure since the guest isn't sure when the coin went missing. David was here part of the day yesterday and today. He left immediately after the last act today."

"He did?"

Liz's heart sank. "That doesn't mean he stole it." But she couldn't help remembering several other odd incidents involving him that weekend, including a less-than-satisfactory answer about why he'd gone up to the third floor after being asked to stay on the ground floor.

"I'll need your guest's full name," Houghton said, "and his home address."

"His name is Jeremy Nichols." She rummaged through a file folder and read off his address in Terre Haute.

"Jeremy Nichols?" The line was quiet for a moment. "He doesn't write those police procedurals, does he?"

"Yes, he does actually. Have you read them?"

"Only a couple. The men here like them. There's usually a beat-up paperback of his in the break room. I didn't know he was still writing."

"Yes, but I get the impression that he's no longer *selling* much."

"Is that so?" He tapped on the phone in a staccato rhythm. "Well, tell everyone to sit tight, and I'll be over there in ten minutes."

"Thanks."

"No problem."

He was as good as his word. Ten minutes after hanging up, he entered the inn's foyer where Liz waited for him.

"Everyone's still here," she said. "Do you want to question them all?"

"I may need to in a while, but they can wait in their rooms if they like. I'll talk to Jeremy first. Could you ask him to come down?"

"Sure."

Two minutes later, Liz led Jeremy into the kitchen. She could be wrong, but Liz sensed that his swaggering bravado was nothing but show, and that apprehension lurked just beneath the skin. Why? Was he surprised that she'd involved the police?

Chief Houghton was installed at the kitchen table. "Here, have a seat." He nodded at Jeremy as he pushed out a chair opposite with his foot. Then he flipped to a clean page of his notebook. "I'll need some details in order to file a report, Mr. Nichols. By the way, your books are real popular down at the station."

"Thank you." Jeremy preened like a peacock. As if by magic, all traces of agitation disappeared, and he sat down.

Houghton glanced up at Liz. "Any chance of getting a cup of coffee?"

"Sure. Won't take a minute." Liz wondered why Houghton was acting so casual about the whole thing, as if he was making a social call. Was he really as impressed with Jeremy Nichols, the writer, as Jeremy was with himself?

"Now, Mr. Nichols," Chief Houghton said, "tell me about this coin."

Jeremy launched into a description that made his good luck piece sound like a treasure that should have been guarded with the crown jewels.

"I assume, as valuable as it sounds, that you had the good sense to insure it."

"Of course, but I would prefer to have it back."

"Naturally." The chief capped his pen and took a big gulp of the coffee Liz set at his elbow. "The thing is, Mr. Nichols, I did a background check on you before heading over here. You filed for bankruptcy recently. You were also charged with insurance fraud two years ago."

"That was never proved!" Jeremy protested.

"No, but the insurance company didn't pay out either. They must have been convinced that there was something fishy about your claim."

"Well, there wasn't." He stood abruptly and leaned over the table, his face close to the chief's. "And my gold coin *was* stolen here."

Houghton didn't move a muscle.

Liz felt obligated to speak up. "Several other guests also saw his coin this weekend. He did have it here."

"See?" Jeremy said, sitting back down.

The chief leaned back, then nodded as if he'd made a decision. "I think we'll continue this discussion down at the station. Get your wallet and ID. You can ride with me."

Jeremy's face blanched. "Is that really necessary? I only want to file a theft report."

"Yes, and you can," Houghton agreed affably. "But first, let's be certain that the item is missing and not just—shall we say—mislaid?"

The atmosphere in the kitchen was thick as fog. Jeremy and the chief stared at each other, taking each other's measure.

Jeremy broke first. "All right, all right. It's just—I mean—I'm only short of cash temporarily."

Liz jerked back. "So you're saying that insurance fraud helps you make ends meet until the economy picks up?"

"Fine. I still have the coin."

"Let's see it," Houghton said.

Jeremy reached below the table and untied his shoe, then took it off. Sliding his fingers inside, he pulled out the infamous gold coin. The chief held out his hand, palm up, and Jeremy deposited it there.

"Hmm. You don't get a lot for $3,500 these days, do you?" Houghton held it out for Liz to see.

She agreed. It didn't look like much. In fact, even if she bit it hard like she'd seen in old-time Westerns, she suspected no tooth mark would show.

"It's worth every penny," Jeremy said. "I can prove it. I've had it appraised."

Liz held it up to the light. "You may have had an appraisal done on a similar-looking gold coin, but it wasn't for this one, was it?"

Silence hung on so long this time that Liz almost had to bite her tongue to keep from rushing in to fill the void.

Finally, Jeremy's shoulders slumped. "Okay, you got me, but you can't blame a guy for trying."

"Actually, I can," the chief replied mildly. "Attempted fraud and wasting police time is against the law. You can be charged."

Liz nodded as the pieces fell into place. "You undoubtedly had a real gold coin at one time, and you have an authentic appraisal of the genuine coin, right?"

Looking thoroughly defeated, Jeremy nodded without looking up.

"So," Houghton said, picking up the story, "he decided to have the substitute coin 'stolen' this weekend where no one would suspect him, not with you having a real pickpocket taking things as part of the mystery game. After filing a report with me, he would be free to go home and file an insurance claim based on the old appraisal." He leaned forward suddenly, making Jeremy jump. "But you already sold the genuine coin before coming here, didn't you?"

Jeremy nodded again, his eyes on his hands. "Now what?" His voice was barely discernible.

The chief let the silence drag on while he was apparently considering his options. "Pack up and go home, Mr. Nichols," he said. "And please don't let me see your face again unless it's on the back cover of a new book."

Jeremy didn't have to be told twice. He took off, and his steps running up the staircase echoed in the rotunda.

They chatted briefly, and then Liz walked Houghton to the front door. She caught a glimpse of her reflection in the foyer glass and was surprised at how good she looked in the Victorian gown. She'd been so preoccupied with her demanding guests all weekend that she'd had little chance to appreciate the exquisite gift Mary Ann and Sadie had sewn for her. She really should thank them again. It wouldn't hurt her guests to sit and sweat a little longer.

She headed toward the Sew Welcome Shop, where Sadie was holding down the fort.

"Hey there," Liz called.

Sadie glanced up from a scrapbook she was studying. "Why, Liz, don't you look elegant, if I do say so myself." She scooted from behind the counter. "Go on. Twirl in a circle. Let me see the complete effect."

Laughing, Liz whirled for her, then glided up and down the store, giving Sadie the full treatment of the way that the blouse molded to her while the skirt flowed around her. "The outfit makes me feel graceful and stylish. It perked me up wearing it this weekend, and believe me, I needed perking up."

"I noticed the police car parked in the drive. Tough weekend?"

"If you only knew." Liz glanced into the rotunda and lowered her voice. "I'll tell you about it later. How's Mary Ann doing?"

"She's had a tough weekend too."

"How's the sprained ankle?"

"She had a painful night, and it felt even worse this morning and was *so* swollen." She pulled up her pants leg to demonstrate. "It turned purple all around this area. I took one look at it this morning and bundled her and all three boys into my car, and off we went to the ER."

"What did they say?"

"It was just a sprain, not a fracture. But she has to stay off it for a couple of weeks."

"That's terrible!"

"It's been so slow in here this afternoon that I think I'll put a sign in the window and close up early. Mary Ann said not to, but I'll feel better being there till the boys are picked up. They're good kids, but busy. I beat them at Monopoly last night, so they've challenged me to a rematch today."

"But no soccer?"

"No soccer." Sadie laughed and motioned Liz over to the worktable where a photo album was open. "This afternoon I've just been thumbing through old photos instead of sweeping and dusting like I'd planned."

Liz leaned over the open photo album, glad that her friends were dependable about capturing special times and projects the old-fashioned way. So few people put actual photos in albums anymore, but Liz loved turning each page of pictures. It wasn't the same feeling when someone showed her a photo on their phone.

The more Liz looked at the photos, the more peaceful she felt. Many were photos of the projects made by the Material Girls. Most of the quilts had been donated or auctioned off for a good cause, but Liz was glad someone had thought to capture the memory first.

Mary Ann and Sadie had also included photos of authentic Amish quilts sold at the craft shows and consignment stores. When she turned another page, she found photos of half a dozen faceless Amish dolls.

Liz stared at them, mesmerized. She'd always been intrigued by them. One day she'd try her hand at making one. She knew the shop sold patterns for making all sizes, from old bearded men dolls to little girl dolls holding their own faceless baby dolls.

"Liz?"

She jumped. "What?"

"Are you all right?" Sadie taped her sign in the shop window. "It's like you froze."

Liz laughed shortly. "My brain is fried. After things calm down for all of us, I'll tell you about the weekend." She tapped a picture with her fingernail. "I think I'd like to sew one of these."

Sadie pointed at a display on a table near the window. "Look at those. They're on loan to us from your Sarah."

In wooden beds covered by miniature quilts sat three dolls. Liz reached out and squeezed a cloth arm.

"That one's stuffed with straw," Sadie said. "And that one's stuffed with quilt batting. The biggest one is stuffed with rags."

Each body was made from unbleached muslin. Dressed in dark clothing and bonnets, the dolls somehow cast a spell over Liz.

Thoughtfully she fingered one of the aprons. Something about them stirred a longing in her for a simpler life, the kind her mother had grown up with but had left long before Liz was in the picture. Since moving to Pleasant Creek, Liz had found many aspects of the lifestyle appealing. The Amish weren't just peaceful and unrushed. They also didn't appear to compete with each other. Liz couldn't imagine any of them feeling the pressure she'd felt all weekend, trying to entertain crabby guests or agonizing about what a reviewer might say about her. The Amish seemed to have no pecking order. No one was better than the others. They didn't have to perform or prove anything.

And yet, the Amish had their own challenges. Liz thought about the woman whose buggy had been run off the road. That made her think of David and how he'd followed her, how Liz had seen him at the lake with an Amish woman, and how evasive he'd been about being on the third floor.

Sadie grabbed her bag and jingled her car keys. Liz followed her out into the rotunda and waved goodbye. She should probably go tell her guests they were free to go.

Liz sighed. If only she had a couple of free hours to walk and sort out her jumbled thoughts. This weekend had held more mysteries than she had planned.

17

After changing into jeans and a sweater, and hanging up her Victorian skirt and blouse, Liz removed her cameo earrings, combed her hair, and slipped on a sturdy pair of shoes. As she left her quarters, she glanced up to see Penny struggling to carry two large suitcases down the stairs.

"Here, let me help you." Liz ran up half the flight to take one of the suitcases.

"Thank you," Penny said, puffing a little. "You'd think they wouldn't be so heavy going down the stairs."

"You'd think so," Liz agreed. "I'll carry this one out to the car for you."

After grabbing a jacket, Liz headed to the parking lot behind the inn and loaded the luggage into the trunk of Penny's silver four-door sedan.

Head down against the wintry chill, Penny followed Liz back inside. "Before I collect Mother, let me say that I'm sorry if her condition and her fears caused extra problems this weekend." Tears welled in her eyes, but she blinked them back. "You were very kind to me about my diary. Thank you for getting it back to me."

"No problem. Really." Liz touched her arm. "I understand. And if I find Louise's jewelry, I'll mail it right away."

"Thank you. I guess we should be on our way. I promised to buy Mother some Amish bread and rolls on the way home."

In a few minutes Penny was back, assisting her mother down the staircase. Liz watched them slowly descend. Louise looked tired, but none the worse for wear. For someone who'd had recent heart surgery, she handled the stairs quite well. Liz hoped and prayed, for both Rollins ladies' sakes, that the dementia could be treated and slowed down with the proper medication. They deserved to enjoy many happy years together yet.

With one of them holding onto each of Louise's arms, they steered her over the slick parking lot. Liz took smaller steps to match Louise's. The gravel was slippery after the snow had thawed yesterday, then refrozen into ice in the night.

Soon both mother and daughter were buckled in and waving goodbye, and Liz gratefully watched them go. They turned north toward the Amish settlement, where they should find plenty of home bakeries open, even on a Sunday afternoon. More than likely, they'd find an Amish child or teen acting as clerk today.

As Liz watched them disappear around a bend in the road, she debated between stripping beds that night or leaving all the rooms until tomorrow when Sarah would return to help her. She was tired and quickly decided the rooms could wait. Since her reviewer wasn't coming tomorrow after all, she had no one to prepare for till later in the week.

Starting back across the icy gravel toward the utility room door, she was startled by a loud *thump*, like someone hitting the window with a snowball. She glanced upward, expecting to see that another bird had flown blindly into the glass. She saw nothing, though, and moved on.

Thump.

There it was again. Was someone knocking on the glass? She scanned the windows on the ground floor, but they were empty. She backed up and peered at the second floor, scanning those windows as well. Nothing again.

This time she stood and waited, jacket pulled tightly around her, and shivered in the frigid breeze. *Thump*! Backing up even further, she stared up at the third-floor windows of the empty rooms where Penny and her mother had stayed. No movement. Nothing.

Liz waited another minute until she heard it again. Unless it was a trick of the light, she thought she spotted something in the third-floor window. It disappeared before she could determine if it was just a reflection.

But then she heard a louder *thump* at the same time she saw a movement. Someone must be inside, throwing something at the window. Was it to get her attention? But why?

She started inside, wondering who could be up there. The second-floor guests were still in the inn, but if one of them wanted her attention, they'd simply come get her. They wouldn't climb to the third floor and throw things at the window without showing their faces. So who could be up there?

Then her heart skipped a beat, followed by a fierce pounding. Her mind raced ahead of her, piecing together unrelated fragments of information and snippets of memory that raced through her mind.

David holding a burned note from a guest accusing him of murder. David descending from the third floor, but refusing to give her a plausible explanation. David departing in a hurry this afternoon, without a word, just leaving a note with his costume. Had he really rushed off to work?

Or had he even left the building at all?

She grabbed her phone and looked up the number of the hospital, then called and asked for the cafeteria. "Is David Mills there, please?"

"No, he's not." The voice was gruff and irritated. "He's over an hour late."

Liz heard another *thump* and hung up. She glanced at the

third-floor window in time to see what looked like a foot hitting the glass before it slid down and out of sight.

She slipped and slid across the icy gravel to get inside. *Hang on, David, I'm coming.*

Inside, Liz took the steps to the top floor, two at a time, around and around the staircase. *Please let me be in time!* On the third floor, she rattled the knob of the Sunset Room. It was locked.

Penny must have locked it when leaving before turning in their keys.

"David? Can you hear me?" She pounded on the door. No answer. "I'll be right back!"

Liz raced back downstairs and grabbed the duplicate keys for the top floor, then again raced up the stairs. At the top, she bent double to catch her breath. Gasping, she breathed deeply until the pressure in her chest eased. Then, stumbling across the landing to the room Penny had occupied, she inserted her duplicate key into the lock.

Her hand shook as she worked the key. "Come on, come on," she said, twisting it back and forth. When the key finally turned, she flung open the door.

And found no one.

Then a moan floated up from the other side of the bed. Liz raced around the foot of the bed and gasped. David lay beneath the window overlooking the parking lot. His mouth was covered with duct tape. His hands were bound together with the same tape. A head wound had bled copiously, but appeared to have stopped and the blood dried. How long had he lain here? Since eleven thirty when Liz had found his costume and note and assumed he'd left?

A fireplace poker—one she recognized from the library—lay beside him, the sharp end covered in blood. More blood had run down the side of his temple and soaked into the bright yellow rag rug. It was already turning brown.

His eyes opened, filled with panic. Liz dropped to her knees beside him, but David closed his eyes again, either in relief or pain. Or maybe he'd passed out. Or maybe he'd—

I can't even think that.

She turned at the noise in the hallway and peered up over the bed. The four remaining guests stared at her from the door. Had one of them done this horrible thing? Liz took a deep breath to calm her thinking. *Don't be silly.* No guest but Penny, or maybe her mother, had had access to this room. Judging from the drying blood, David had lain there for a good hour or maybe more, including the time when Penny had packed up to leave and locked the door behind her.

"Help me here. David has been hurt."

They rushed into the room and gathered at the end of the bed. Cherise gasped and claimed she was going to faint. Pushing her aside, Liz ordered Drew to call 911 and ask for both police and ambulance to come to the inn. Liz raced to the bathroom located between the bedrooms and grabbed nail scissors.

When she returned, Jeremy spoke from the foot of the bed. "Elevate his head above his heart. Having his wound on the same level as his pumping heart might make the bleeding start up again."

What he said sounded like common sense. She should have known that.

"Here, Vivian, help me." Liz moved closer to the window so Vivian could crouch down beside her. Grabbing two pillows off the bed, Liz gently raised David's head and Vivian put the pillows underneath. "I'm going to cut the tape from his mouth so he can breathe easier," Liz said.

Willing David to open his eyes again, she snipped bit by bit, careful not to cut him. She leaned over him as soon as she pulled the pieces of duct tape off, listening for his breath.

She heard nothing.

Turning her face to place her cheek near his mouth, she waited. It was faint, but she definitely felt a tiny burst of warm breath on her skin.

Cherise leaned over and picked up a piece of paper lying half under David's leg. She read it and frowned. "Liz, did you see this?"

"No, what is it?"

Cherise held it out for her to read. Written on another piece of Sherlock Holmes notepaper, the cryptic message simply said, *an eye for an eye for my dead brother.*

What in heaven's name does that mean?

She tucked the note in her pocket. Because David was lying next to Penny's bed, Liz assumed that Penny must have written it. She had struck him hard enough that he would require stitches, but hopefully not hard enough to kill him. So why was her attack "an eye for an eye" for someone who was dead?

Drew hung up. "Police are on their way and should be here in a couple minutes. An ambulance will be coming from further away, but with the highways clear, it will only be another five or ten minutes."

Liz nodded. "Thank you."

David moved his head and groaned. He pushed Vivian away and tried to sit up. Before Liz could stop him, his eyes closed again, and he fell back to the floor.

Liz fought the urge to cry out. Was David dead? Or just overcome by pain? Had she been too late to save him?

18

At the sound of the police siren, Liz stood then flew down the stairs.

Standing on the front porch wasn't Chief Houghton as she'd expected. Instead, the officer was someone she didn't know, who looked like a recruit fresh from the academy.

"Come in, officer," Liz said. "The man who got attacked is on the third floor. We called an ambulance too."

He thanked her and started up the stairs at a good clip. Liz started to follow. "Ma'am, can you wait here and direct the EMTs when they arrive?"

"I'll bring them right up."

She ran out on the porch and waited in the cold. If only Pleasant Creek had its own hospital and ambulance.

A few minutes later, she heard the siren before the ambulance turned the corner two blocks away. Lights flashing, it raced down the street and stopped in front of the inn. Two EMTs jumped out. Pushing the wheeled stretcher and carrying first-responder bags, they hurried up the walk.

"This way," Liz said, holding the door. "Straight up the stairs to the third floor. The officer is already there." She pointed, amazed at how calm her voice sounded when her own pulse was racing. *Please hurry!*

After a brief conversation, one of the EMTs went back to the ambulance for a backboard. They would use it to bring David down to the wheeled stretcher waiting in the rotunda. With their bags and the backboard, they moved swiftly up the staircase with Liz right behind them.

Upstairs, the guests were asked to wait on the landing, but to keep access to the stairs clear. After the EMTs examined David, checking vitals and starting some kind of fluid dripping into his veins, they lifted him onto the backboard. Liz was grateful to see his eyes open, but he didn't respond to the EMTs' questions.

Carrying David down the stairs was a slow process, but once they were in the rotunda, it was simpler. By the time David was rolled on the stretcher to the ambulance, his eyes were closed again. Whether from the pain of being jostled or passing out, Liz didn't know.

Lights flashed as the ambulance pulled away from the curb, and soon the sirens were blaring again. The ambulance whipped away out of sight, and Liz sent up a silent prayer for David.

"Ma'am?" The young police officer tapped her arm. "I need to ask you a few questions."

"Certainly." Liz focused on his face, then his badge, trying to get the image of David's face out of her mind. "How can I help you?"

"I've talked to the four remaining guests, but tell me again about the key arrangement and why you believe the assailant had to be—" he consulted his notepad "—Penny Rollins."

Liz explained the schedule for the day, when she'd last seen David, how each guest had a key only to his or her own room, and, according to the EMTs, David had undoubtedly already been injured and lying behind the bed for over an hour—during the time Penny was packing up to leave. "She locked her room when checking out, which was unusual, but no doubt she didn't want anyone going in there until she got away. She was the only one with the opportunity."

"Do you have the make and model of Penny Rollins's car?"

"Yes, let me get the registration list." She went to the kitchen and grabbed the file of papers off her desk. "Here it is. And here's her license plate number too."

"Very good. We'll get an APB out." He copied the information, then got on his phone and repeated the information. He waited, then said, "Thanks. Not surprised." He turned to Liz. "The license plate number was a fake. No such plate. Are the make, model and year listed correct?"

Liz shrugged, feeling sheepish. "It was a silver four-door, but I don't recognize makes and models, let alone years." She bit her lower lip. "I do know that they headed down the road toward the Amish community though. Something about picking up some baked goods on the way home."

"I expect that was just a ruse," the officer said. "I'm guessing she cut across to the highway as soon as she was out of sight. No one's going to hang around bakery shopping before escaping the scene of their crime."

Liz nodded. That made sense. "Wait, I forgot something." She reached into her pocket for the note Cherise had picked up near the body. "This was found with David."

The officer read it. "'An eye for an eye for my dead brother'? Any idea what that means?"

"No, I'm afraid not."

He added the scrap of paper to his notebook, which he tucked into his breast pocket, and said, "We'll be in touch."

After the officer left, Liz hurried into the kitchen. Too traumatized to even put on a pot of coffee, she collapsed in the breakfast nook. Shivering, she hugged herself, thinking again about the note found by David's body. What did Penny have against David? What was bad enough to seriously injure him?

Liz's mind ran in circles but got nowhere, like revving a car engine while stuck in park. What was the connection between David and Penny? Why did she want "an eye for an eye" revenge? What had he ever done to her? Had Penny caught him snooping? If so, why hadn't she said anything? Or had he surprised her, and she lashed out in self-defense? And what did that cryptic note mean anyway?

She held herself motionless, willing her mind to slow down and think logically. She waited. Then, one by one, several pieces of information and fragments of memories fell into place—and clicked. *Of course.*

Racing to her laptop, Liz hunted for the articles she'd started to read earlier when she got interrupted. Her search for *death at magic show* brought up the original article she'd read about David Miller. In that article, freshly written after the sudden death on stage, the name of the victim had been withheld pending notification of kin. She scrolled down further to a follow-up article written two days later.

And there she found it. A photo of the victim and the name underneath: Ronald Rollins. His bio said he was survived in death by his mother, Louise, and his sister, Penny.

Liz closed her laptop and leaped to her feet. It made sense now, a sickening sense. Penny's "eye for an eye" couldn't have referred to David. She wouldn't have left him alive if it had. But the note might very well mean she intended to kill a family member of David's because—intentional or not—he had killed a family member of hers. And who would that be?

And then Liz knew. David Mills—no, Miller—must be the son of Rhoda Miller, the woman he'd followed and later met down at the lake.

If she was right about Penny targeting a family member, Liz needed help immediately. Penny already had such a head start.

Liz called Houghton to tell him. He was in conference with someone, so she left a message. "It's urgent," she stressed to the desk sergeant. "Please see that he gets it as soon as possible. It truly may be life or death."

She couldn't wait for his returned call, or it could be too late. Yet she didn't want to go alone.

Jackson.

She placed the call, waiting impatiently for him to answer. It went to voicemail. "Jackson? It's Liz. I need help, and I think one of my guests—"

He picked up. "Liz? It's Jackson. Sorry I didn't get to the phone. What's going on?"

As quickly and succinctly as possible, Liz told him about finding David injured and bound in Penny's room after they'd left. "Her car went in the direction of the Amish community, and I think her 'eye for an eye' threat means she's going to injure someone Amish."

"Why would she do that? That doesn't make sense."

Tears of frustration welled up. There was no time to explain. Penny could already have killed someone.

"Please, just come. I need your help, and I'll explain on the way. But hurry."

"I'll be right there."

Liz grabbed her winter jacket and was waiting on the sidewalk when Jackson's truck pulled up at the curb. She climbed in the cab and buckled up.

"Head toward the Miller farm, the one that's just past Miriam's and around the first corner. There's a sign by the road advertising faceless Amish dolls for sale."

She launched into as concise a summary of events as she could. Jackson listened, occasionally glancing at her or asking a quick question to clarify something.

"That's why I think Penny is out to kill a relative of David's."

"You're sure David Mills is really David Miller?"

"Yes. If you'd seen the photo from the account of the magic show death, you'd be sure too."

She also reported how she'd spotted David following an Amish woman old enough to be his mother from the Sew Welcome Shop. "And Rhoda could easily have been the same woman I saw him with by the lake."

Jackson pushed the speed limit driving to the Miller farm. "What did you say the magician's stage name was?"

"The Great Shima," Liz said. "What does Shima mean? Do you know?"

Jackson glanced in the rearview mirror. "I doubt if it means anything, but think about the letters in the name. Rearrange them. What does it spell?"

S-H-I-M-A. S-H-I-M-A. *A-M-I-S-H.* "He kept his Amish ties through his stage name."

"It looks that way."

"And the doll maker must be his mother. I wonder if the young woman riding in the buggy with her when it was run off the road could be David's sister. I've seen the two women together at craft shows sometimes." She thought back to the day Rhoda's buggy had been sideswiped. "David was really scared the day they were forced off the road. I wondered at the time how he knew instinctively to handle the horse and stop it from bolting."

"Who ran her off the road?"

"I don't know. Some tourist who didn't even have the decency to stop. It was a drizzly day and—"

"What?"

"It all happened so fast that day. I didn't get a good look at the car. But I remember that it was silver, midsize. And Penny drives a silver sedan."

Liz hunched forward as they drove, fighting rolling waves of self-blame. If only she'd followed up on this earlier. If only she'd confronted David about the threatening note right away. She could have convinced him to go to the police. Maybe she should have reported it herself.

A minute later they rounded the curve past Miriam's farmhouse. Liz had been there dozens of times to visit Miriam and to buy eggs, butter, and meat. The Miller farm was nearby. Liz strained to see through the windbreak trees and up the lane into their farmyard. The truck bounced over the frozen ruts in the drive. They passed a windmill not far from the house that turned slowly in the breeze, casting its shadow over a red barn. Acres of farmland stretched beyond it, waiting for the planting of spring crops.

"There's her car. And that's her mother out in the yard." She leaned forward, palms braced on the dash. "I don't see Penny anywhere. Do you?"

"No."

When they stopped, Liz hopped out of the cab and approached Louise with caution. "Are you all right, Louise? It's me, Liz. Why don't you come sit in our warm truck?"

Louise jerked her arm away. "I don't want to."

"It's too cold to stand around outside."

Out of the corner of her eye, Liz watched Jackson stride to the craft shop attached to the side of the house. He tried to go inside, but the door was locked.

Louise laughed, a sound so foreign and abrasive that Liz jerked back. "He won't find Penny in there."

"Where is she then?"

Louise turned in a slow circle in the frozen yard. "I don't know! Where is she?" She grabbed Liz's arm. "You're too late."

A chill raced down Liz's spine, and she knew it wasn't from the cold wind blowing across the open field.

Leaving Louise in the snowy yard, Liz ran toward the front of the house with Jackson on her heels. He signed to her that he was going around to try to enter through the back of the house. She nodded that she understood and moved close to the front window, crouching beneath it.

She rose up slowly to peer over the window ledge. What met her eyes made her blood curdle.

Rhoda Miller was backed into a corner of a living room, while Penny brandished a metal rod in her face. Was that a tire iron? Liz started to cry out, but she sensed Louise's presence before she actually heard her footsteps crunch on the snow behind her. Liz whipped around as Louise swung a piece of firewood, aimed at her temple. Liz screamed, and an answering shout came from inside. Had Mrs. Miller been struck?

Liz instinctively flung up her forearm to shield her face, and her arm took the brunt of the attack. She grabbed the stick of wood from Louise, who began to scream.

"Penny! Help me!"

The door flew open and Penny stood in the entry, eyes wild, gray braid loose. Somewhere at the back of the house, glass shattered, and there was the sound of wood splintering. Penny charged at Liz, but Jackson appeared right behind Penny. He snatched the tire iron from her and threw it, then pinned Penny's arms to her sides. Liz had Louise in the same kind of grip, but the woman fought like someone much younger. She wasn't nearly as frail as she had appeared.

Liz's arm throbbed, and she hoped it wasn't broken. She raised her voice and called out, "Mrs. Miller? Are you all right?"

The Amish woman appeared in her doorway. "*Dänka, ja.* She missed me. I can be quick when I must be."

Liz nearly cried when she heard the welcome siren of a police car. A moment later, it pulled into the Miller driveway, lights flashing. Liz let Jackson explain the situation to Chief Houghton while Officer Jack Gerst put the Rollins women into the back seat of the squad car.

Liz went indoors with Rhoda. "I need to tell you something.

David Mills is in the hospital, or he should be by now. I have reason
to believe that he's your son."

She grabbed Liz's arm. "Ja, he's my *Sön*. What happened to him?"

"He was attacked by that woman who threatened you. She hit him
in the head with a poker, and it probably needed stitches. It happened
at my inn a short while ago. I believe that this woman came to Pleasant
Creek specifically to look for your son."

"Did he tell you she was coming here?"

Liz paused. "No, I guessed she was heading this way."

Rhoda scrutinized Liz's face. "Did my Sön tell you anything?"

"I'm afraid not," Liz admitted. "He was unconscious. He'd lost
a lot of blood."

"I'll get my coat." Quietly, but with trembling fingers, Rhoda
buttoned her long wool coat and pulled on thick woolen mittens. "I
will go to the hospital with Ruth Yoder. She is just up the road. She
will want to go."

"We'd be glad to drive you both. The truck can go faster."

"The *Valga*—er, the buggy—will make it."

Surprised, Liz realized Rhoda was particularly strict in her beliefs,
compared to many of the Amish. Liz wondered if Ruth was the young
woman she'd seen talking to Mrs. Miller a few times. A daughter
maybe? It would be common for her married daughter to live nearby.

"May I at least drive you to Ruth's home?"

She barely hesitated. "Ja, this is an emergency."

Liz borrowed Jackson's keys. "I'll be back in five minutes," she said.

On the way to the next farm to the north, Liz sensed that Rhoda,
with eyes closed, was . . . praying. When they pulled into the driveway
of the Yoder farm, Rhoda thanked her warmly for coming to her rescue.

Liz had been back at the Miller farm only five minutes when she
saw a buggy carrying two Amish women fly by at top speed. David's

family would be with him soon. She hoped that they would be met with good news when they arrived.

Turning, Liz shuddered when she caught the malevolent glare coming from the back seat of the squad car.

19

"Could you please follow us to the police station?" Houghton asked Liz and Jackson. "I need to interview Penny Rollins without Louise. I can't tell if her mother is really ill or if it's an act. It seems to come and go, but that can be common with certain ailments."

"How can we help?" Liz asked.

"Louise knows you, Liz," he said. "If you could sit with her in the waiting area, get her some coffee or a snack, anything, it would keep her calmer than having a stranger, and a policeman at that, take charge of her."

"You're right. I'd be glad to help."

"I'll come too," Jackson said.

He'd be good to have along. He had a way with the ladies, no matter what their age.

As they pulled out of the Miller driveway, Liz put in a call to the hospital emergency room, asking for David Mills's status. Since she wasn't a relative, she didn't get much information. Liz understood the laws about protecting patients' privacy, but it was frustrating all the same.

"No news?" Jackson asked.

"They're not telling me anything."

"At least he's alive, and that's the main thing right now." He reached over and patted her arm.

"True."

They arrived right behind the chief at the station. He showed Liz and Jackson to a room with a couch and easy chairs and a snack machine while his officers brought in the Rollinses. Louise was led into the room where Jackson and Liz were, while Penny was escorted on. The chief spoke quietly. "If you can keep Louise in here, that would be best."

While Jackson guided Louise to choose three treats from the snack machine, Liz followed Chief Houghton back out into the hallway. "If Jackson watches Louise, could I listen to your interview?"

He shook his head. "You know I can't have you in the interview room."

"Yes, but don't you have two-way mirrors where people can watch without being seen?"

"Like in the TV cop shows?" He raised an eyebrow.

"It might be helpful to you if I listen in. If she lies about something that happened this weekend, I could tell you."

"That's a good point." He pulled at his chin. "Let's do it."

Liz let Jackson know where she'd be. "It's down the hall around the corner. If Louise gives you any trouble or gets frightened, come get me."

"We'll be fine. I bought her a couple of candy bars, so we're friends for life."

Liz rolled her eyes. "I guess the way to a woman's heart is chocolate as long as she lives. Thanks for doing this."

She hurried along behind the police chief and stood where he showed her. Penny paced like a caged animal around the small interview room. It was fascinating to see the chief enter the interview room to join Penny, knowing she could see and hear them, but they couldn't see or hear her.

It began predictably enough, after a recorder was turned on, with Houghton asking Penny if she wanted an attorney present. He said he wasn't arresting her, but he needed to ask her a few questions.

"I don't need a lawyer. I haven't done anything wrong."

"That's fine."

The chief asked routine questions, and Penny gave her name and address and why she'd come to Pleasant Creek. She talked at length about following the mystery clues, dressing up as Sherlock Holmes, and the bit of shopping she and her mother had done at a craft fair.

Houghton waited till she trailed off. "The mystery weekend was only a cover for your real reason for being here, wasn't it?"

For several minutes, Penny tried to get around the question, waxing eloquent in her descriptions of the clues and actors and how she'd solved the whodunit before anyone else.

Chief Houghton continued to listen, then asked another probing question, one after the other. Penny ignored them all, but after ten minutes, Liz could see how edgy she was.

It wasn't until Houghton changed the subject that she cracked. "Let's talk about your brother's death," he said. "Natural causes, I heard."

At that, Penny jumped out of her chair, knocking it over as she leaped across the table. "You take that back!" she screamed. "My brother was *murdered*, and you stinkin' cops wouldn't do a thing about it." Liz winced at the expletives lacing her speech as she ranted, but Houghton looked unmoved. Undoubtedly he had heard worse.

"I wasn't there eight years ago when your brother died," Chief Houghton said softly in response to her raving.

"You're all the same though. I tried over and over to get the police to investigate further. My poor mother tried and tried, and it aged her overnight. The coroner refused to change his verdict from natural causes when it was so clearly murder. The magic trick was too simple to cause anyone's death. Don't you understand? It *had* to be murder!" she wailed.

"I want to understand," Houghton said. "Explain it to me."

"I tried other ways to see justice done. I did." She stifled a sob. "I filed a civil suit against David Mills after they refused to hold a criminal trial. I lost. It got dropped for lack of evidence. How could I get the evidence I needed? I'm not a police force or a private investigator or a CSI team."

"Of course not. No one expected that of you."

Liz watched Penny relax a fraction of an inch. She righted her chair and sank back into it. Then, almost as if a spigot had been opened, Penny's story gushed out. Chief Houghton seemed so empathetic to her plight, so calm and understanding, that she dropped her antagonistic stance.

"Mother expected it of me. She said over and over that it was up to me to get justice for my brother if the police refused to." She stifled another sob, but it erupted into a choking sound that tore at Liz's heart. "It took such a toll on Mother. Even after she survived her heart surgery, I could tell it had affected her mind."

"In what way?" Chief Houghton asked, concern evident in his face, body language, and voice.

He's good at this. He really is.

Liz watched as if, almost by magic, Penny subtly morphed into someone else. "My poor mother. Her mental state deteriorated. She became forgetful, even heard and saw things that weren't there."

Liz frowned. That didn't sound like the woman who'd stayed in her inn all weekend. On the other hand, Liz supposed that Penny could have covered for Louise when she forgot things. And there was that episode of Louise swearing she'd seen someone peering through her keyhole, yet when Liz had checked the rooms, there hadn't been anyone there. Maybe Louise *did* imagine things.

Or maybe Penny had planted the idea of the Peeping Tom in her mother's head and staged the whole thing.

In the interview room, Penny stared at her lap for a minute. "Mother is my last close relative—my only sibling and my father are dead—and I see her gradually losing her mental ability. Dementia, the doctors said. Soon I'll be alone in the world."

"How difficult for you." The chief jotted a couple of notes, then slid the box of tissues across the table. "Can I get you some water, Penny? Or tea?"

"No, I'm fine."

Liz got the distinct impression that even if Penny had wanted something, she wasn't about to lose this oh-so-sympathetic listener, even briefly. After years of being the primary caregiver for her mother, it must be balm to her soul to have someone show an interest in her struggles. And despite being there in an official capacity, Liz believed Houghton honestly did care. But that didn't mean he was duped. Liz didn't believe that for a minute. But part of her, the detached part, enjoyed watching him in action. *What a perfect combination of empathy and shrewdness.*

"So let's fast-forward eight years since your brother's death to this weekend," Houghton said. "How did you find out that David Mills would be performing at the inn this weekend?"

Penny clapped her hands like a gleeful child. "I didn't know until we saw him yesterday!"

The chief frowned. "It's a bit much to believe in that kind of coincidence."

"We knew he'd moved to Pleasant Creek two months ago, but not that he'd be at the inn where we were staying."

"How did you know he'd moved here?"

Penny turned coy then, tilting her head to the side and glancing at Houghton. "A private investigator tracked his move here. This was an odd place to relocate in the middle of nowhere. I told him to keep digging. The PI learned that he actually used to live here and his name had been Miller, that he moved away when he was sixteen, and that he was working in a nearby hospital." She leaned across the table as if to whisper a secret. "My original plan was to take Mother on an emergency trip to the hospital during the weekend. Then I'd find him in the cafeteria and have it out with him. But it turned out I didn't need to do that. I couldn't believe my luck when he came to perform at the inn."

Liz had an immediate flashback to when David had first arrived to pick up his script. Penny and Louise had seemed startled, almost shocked, when they were introduced to him.

"So your plan to get your revenge on this man—"

"Killer," Penny spat.

"—the man you hold responsible for your brother's death," the chief amended. "Your plan was suddenly made easier."

Penny thought about it. "Not easier, but it changed." She dropped her voice. "We thought of a much better revenge than killing him."

"What was that?"

"Letting him live." She grinned then as if she'd said something terribly clever. "What's worse than dying? Living after a close loved one dies, that's what." She folded her arms and leaned back. "We took our time."

"To do what?"

"We followed David. We had hours between the scenes that were acted out to go off and put our clues together. And we did. But our clues had nothing to do with that ridiculous Sherlock Holmes drama." She licked her lips. "We sneaked out and followed him. We said we went shopping or to lunch. Once we even told them we were going to church."

"Did you learn anything by following him?" Houghton asked, sounding in awe of her sleuthing abilities.

She lowered her voice, as if telling him a secret. "Once we saw him talking to a woman who could have been his mother's age. She was selling ugly little Amish dolls at a craft booth. Later, we only had to ask one person to find out who she was. I said we wanted to order a large consignment of those dolls. They said she had her own small store and obligingly told us where she lived. So we would have our revenge. We would kill David Miller's mother like he killed my brother."

"So you discovered where she lived. Then what?" he prompted, as if she wasn't telling him a horrifying story. Liz was sure she couldn't have kept her cool the way Houghton did.

Penny's whole demeanor hardened. Through thin tight lips, she said, "Then *you.*" She pounded the table with her fist. "Why did you have to ruin it? We were so close."

"We?" the chief asked.

Penny pulled back immediately. "What do you mean?"

"You said 'we.' Who is 'we'?"

"I meant *I,*" she amended. "*I* was so close. Mother had nothing to do with it. She didn't realize what my plan was."

"You don't have to shelter her," Houghton said. "I know what it's like. My grandmother had dementia, and she didn't know what she was saying sometimes. We understood, but it was still hard."

Penny studied his innocent-looking face, suspicion clearly written on hers. "I don't have to shelter her? So you're saying if Mother was involved with this, you'd understand that she wasn't in her right mind?"

"People with dementia can't be held responsible for their actions, can they?"

"No, they can't. And my mother is in that category. For the last six months it's grown worse and worse. I've covered for her the best I can, but I can't be with her all the time, can I?" Her eyes darted back and forth as the words tumbled out, and Liz had the feeling that she was making it up as she went along. "I'm glad you understand. I haven't had anyone to talk to about this. Her doctor doesn't explain anything to me. I had to write in a diary just to keep my sanity. You can ask Liz.

She even read part of it and told the other guests to keep an eye out for my mother in case she wandered."

Liz shook her head as she tried to follow Penny's convoluted story. It veered off suddenly in different directions, and she even contradicted herself.

The chief shook his head in sympathy. "Her doctor should have been more help to you. Is he too old to be in practice anymore?"

Liz could almost see the wheels turning in Penny's mind.

"No, her doctor isn't old. I took her to Indiana University's memory clinic twice, before and after her heart surgery. You have no idea how disturbing it is when you see your last relative make out her will. I knew her days were numbered. And I was right. Dr. Lister confirmed that the dementia was advancing faster, and that her medication was doing no good." She reached across the table and grabbed Houghton's hand, then let it go. "I'm so worried about her, but she truly isn't responsible for what she does."

"That reminds me," Chief Houghton said, pushing back his chair. "I'll be right back. I want to check on your mother."

"Where is she?"

"In the break room having a snack," he said. "She seemed quite happy when I left her."

Penny frowned. "Do keep an eye on her. She can be . . . erratic."

"Erratic how?"

"Wild, even violent if she gets frightened," Penny said.

"Has she been violent before?"

"Just minor things," Penny assured him. "Like this weekend, for instance. I surprised her in the kitchen—she was returning a knife she'd borrowed—and she plunged the whole blade into a melon."

Louise had done that? Liz couldn't picture it. Or was that yet another bold-faced lie? Had Penny done it and was now making her mother the scapegoat?

"Thank you for mentioning that," Houghton said. "While I'm in the break room, can I bring you anything back?"

"I missed lunch."

"I'll see what I can find."

He stuck his notebook in his pocket and stepped out of the interview room, pulling the door shut behind him. At the observation window, he asked, "What do you think?"

"She seems as confused sometimes as she claims her mother is. If Louise is that far advanced in her illness, I have to say that she hid it well. Or Penny compensated for her very successfully."

"I want to check on that." He stepped into his office across the hallway.

While she wasn't trying to eavesdrop, Liz could easily overhear the chief tracking down a Dr. Lister at the Indiana University Alzheimer Disease Center. It took ten minutes, and Penny at first fidgeted in her chair, then stood and paced back and forth across the tiny room. When Houghton came back to the observation window, he kept his voice low. "It's what I guessed. The doctor did see Louise Rollins a month ago and did a whole battery of tests, but he pronounced her mentally fit as a fiddle. She's no more confused than you are."

"So, Penny's account—and that diary of six months' worth of sad stories—it's all a big elaborate lie?" Liz cradled her sore arm. "That means Louise knew what she was doing when she attacked me with that firewood."

"Looks that way." He glanced at Penny through the two-way mirror, and his expression hardened. "Guess what else? I asked the doctor if Louise's heart surgery could have affected her thinking. You know, if she was deprived of oxygen during the surgery or something."

"Was she?"

"Turns out that would have been impossible," Houghton said lightly.

"There *was* no heart surgery."

"*What?*"

"No. Louise is probably as fit and sharp as we are."

Liz shook her head with both disbelief and disgust. She'd fallen for every sob story Penny had fed her. "And it sounds like Penny sent the threatening note to David and struck him with the poker, but she plans to blame her mother. That's despicable."

"My guess is that both women planned and executed it, but if Penny can lay the blame at her mother's feet, she will. Penny probably thinks her mother would go to a nursing home instead of jail. Penny would get away with it and no longer have to be solely responsible for her mother to boot."

"But she had to know that someone would call that doctor and check out her story."

"Not necessarily. It's been my experience that criminals on all levels think they're cleverer than they are. She thought by fabricating six months of 'proof in writing' with the diary, then making sure you saw it, that she'd be home free with her story."

Liz shook her head. This woman was unbelievable. "Will you tell her that you called the doctor?"

"Not yet. From what you said when you arrived at the Miller farm, Louise was outside standing guard while Penny went inside to exact her revenge. Since her mother is mentally stable, acting as lookout like that may make her an active accomplice to attempted murder."

"I hadn't thought of that."

"So I'd rather not show my hand just yet." He nodded toward Penny, who was still pacing. "If you hear me say a few strange things—"

"I understand."

He went back in and laid an assortment of snacks on the table. "This is stuff I keep in my office. It's better than what's in the break room."

"You were gone a long time." She sat back down, ripped open a bag of miniature chocolate chip cookies, and popped one in her mouth.

He waited a moment. "I'm afraid that now I have to ask some very difficult questions."

She stiffened and stopped chewing.

He smiled to soften the comment. "David Mills was found wounded on the top floor of the inn. Do you know anything about that?"

Penny watched his face, then started chewing again. Not until she swallowed did she answer. "Is he—um, did he die?"

"I don't know. The last I heard he was taken to the hospital, unconscious. You never know with a head wound if victims will even regain consciousness."

"You're calling *him* the victim?"

"A figure of speech when talking about the wounded. That's all."

"Because you know who the *real* victims are here, don't you?"

Houghton made a note, then asked, "How did David come to be wounded?"

"Mother gets so confused." Penny crumpled the cookie wrapper. "I'd asked him upstairs to watch Mother while I loaded the car and checked out." She licked her lips, obviously concocting her story as it came to her. "When I went back to get Mother, he was lying on the floor all bloody. She'd panicked when she saw a strange man in the room. Who can blame her? It was my fault. I thought she would remember him from seeing him acting in those scenes. Her short-term memory is usually better than that."

"Your mother panicked?"

"Yes, she must have."

The chief's voice took on a steely edge. "And then she ran down two flights of stairs to get a fireplace poker, ran back upstairs, and struck David with it? Did he just wait for her?"

"I don't know!" Penny shouted. Then, more thoughtfully, she added, "No, I guess that didn't happen. The poker was already—" She cut herself off abruptly.

"Already in the room? Because you planned the attack?"

"Planned it? No. Mother and I were terrified all weekend. Strange things were happening. I got it for protection." She leaned nearer. "You have to believe me that he was still breathing when we left. But I had to keep him quiet if he came to. I couldn't risk having Mother blamed and taken away!" Her voice rose to a dramatic wail.

Liz honestly couldn't tell if she was lying outright or was so mentally ill, so consumed by hateful revenge, that she believed her own convoluted story. Liz believed now that Penny hadn't wanted to kill David after all. She'd only wanted to get him out of the way a while, but she'd wanted him to live. Liz was sure of that. Penny wanted David to know the pain of surviving a loved one. And whatever her reasons, she was laying the blame squarely at her mother's feet. Her own mother, who was as mentally sound as anyone else according to her doctor.

No matter how it turned out, Liz felt sick about what had happened to David right in her inn. He'd been lying wounded for more than an hour, and she hadn't even known he was in the building. Why hadn't she followed up with him sooner? If he hadn't managed to hit the window and get her attention, she wouldn't have found him until they started cleaning the rooms on Monday morning. And by then, it probably would have been too late.

How could someone do something like that?

20

Liz was weary when Jackson dropped her off at the inn. She'd called the hospital while still at the police station and learned, with great relief, that David had been stitched up and released into a relative's care.

She smiled at that. *A relative's care.* Now that was a story she'd like to hear. After an hour of listening to one of the most twisted tales she'd ever heard, how nice to learn of a caring mother-child relationship. While it was still unclear if Penny would be charged alone or with Louise, the police chief was convinced that they'd worked together, covered for each other, and would likely both be found in the courts to be guilty of assault or attempted murder.

Inside the inn, the labeled keys on the table in the rotunda showed that three more guests had checked out in her absence. By her calculation, only the reviewer was still in residence.

Oh joy.

Well, she might as well clean up the kitchen while she waited for him to leave. As she closed the door to the foyer, she glanced up the street on this quiet Sunday afternoon and saw something that always brought her peace.

An Amish buggy. That sight coupled with the *clip-clop* of horses' hooves on the cobblestones transported her back in time to a more civilized era.

And she could do with something civilized.

To her surprise, the buggy clattered down the street and slowed to a stop in front of the inn. Liz stepped through the foyer and onto the porch.

Rhoda and her neighbor sat erect on the buggy's bench seat. Liz also caught sight of someone in the back, someone with a bright-white bandage on his head.

Liz hurried down the steps, barely noticing the cold. She was only glad that David was alive and well enough to go home to be nursed.

"Hello," she called before even reaching the sidewalk. "I'm so glad to see you all."

Rhoda nodded. "We wanted to stop by and say dänka for what you and your friend did for us today. We thank *Gött* for you."

"I'm glad we got to your farm in time." Liz leaned into the buggy toward David. "I'm just so sorry about what happened before that. I should have seen—"

"No, don't apologize," he said firmly. "I brought the danger to your home. Not knowingly, but it wasn't your fault at all."

"And so much good has come from it," Rhoda said. "But I forget my manners. This is Ruth Yoder."

The young woman turned so Liz could see her face inside the dark bonnet. The cheerful smile brightened her dress of dark navy blue and her practical black shoes.

Ruth spoke with great poise, but her eyes sparkled. "I want to thank you, too, for helping my good friends today."

Liz nodded, and she spotted the adoring look that David shot the pretty young woman. It wasn't a brotherly look for a sister, but more the longing of a man who was pining for someone. Ruth was clearly not Rhoda's daughter. Was it possible that Ruth was a sweetheart from long ago?

"It's good to meet you, Ruth."

Glad she was still wearing her winter coat, Liz moved close to the buggy out of the frigid wind. The sun on her back was welcome. "Are you really all right?" she asked David.

"The doctor says I will be."

"With a mother's tender loving care," Ruth piped up, eyes dancing. Liz smiled to herself. Those sparkling eyes didn't look very sisterly either.

"I just came from the police station," Liz said. "The police chief got a confession from Penny. And her mother was likely her willing accomplice."

Rhoda turned around to gaze at her son, worry creasing her forehead. "David told us about the woman's brother dying during his magic act."

Ruth touched Rhoda's hand briefly. "I think the woman's grief ate at her so badly that she had to find a way to express it. Even an unhealthy one. I don't think it was about you at all."

"I think you're right," Liz agreed, glad that David had filled them in about the incident. "Penny and her mother first pursued various legal ways to blame David for what the coroner called a death from 'natural causes.' When no one agreed with them that David was to blame, they took matters into their own hands and tracked him down to Pleasant Creek."

"We're grateful that he returned to us," Ruth said quietly. "We forgive her."

Liz couldn't help but wonder why David had left the Amish community in the first place when he and his mother so obviously loved each other and a young woman was carrying a torch for him. Was his story anything like her own mother's had been when she left?

She didn't have to wait long.

Rhoda glanced at David, and he nodded. Turning to Liz, she said, "When he was younger, David was fascinated by a magician's act and learned a few tricks just for fun. He couldn't resist showing off the tricks to his friends."

"Then Father caught me," David said.

"Ja," Rhoda admitted, "and he wanted David disciplined for trying to corrupt his friends."

David took up the story. "I felt I had done nothing wrong since it wasn't magic, just fooling the eyes with sleight of hand. But Father called it trickery and deceit. He was furious for the embarrassment I'd caused the family."

Liz listened for traces of anger or bitterness in David's voice, but found none.

His mother hurried to explain. "My husband was a good man with deep convictions. He said standards must be met. If you cared about your community, then commitment to the rules was important. Otherwise we'd disappear and just melt into the English world that surrounds us. He used to say that 'keeping apart is the glue that keeps us together.' For my husband, it was a crime not to support his principles." She sighed, as if she'd repeated that to herself so often over the years that it was memorized. "But he missed his son till the day he died."

"So you had to leave your family?" Liz asked.

"I wasn't kicked out," David clarified, "but the bishop said I was to be cut off from all community activities, including church, for a lengthy time period. I was hotheaded then. I left before my baptism rather than take his punishment, which I felt was unfair." He glanced sheepishly at his mother. "Things change—feelings change—in sixteen years. I subscribed to an Amish newspaper years ago, and back in August, I read that my father had died." He looked down briefly. "I returned to the area and got a job at the hospital, waiting to find out if there was a chance for me to reunite with my family." He looked at Ruth and added, "And good friends." Then he actually blushed, his white bandage showing up even brighter against his flushed face.

Rhoda straightened on the buggy seat. "I never abandoned my oldest boy in my heart, nor did I stop praying he would someday return." She smoothed her long apron down over her knees. "When David came up to talk to me at the market, I was overjoyed, and we began to make plans." She grinned then. "I even told him his old sweetheart had spurned all advances during the sixteen years he'd been gone, praying that one day he would return."

This time it was Ruth's turn to blush furiously. So she *was* a former sweetheart from his teens. Liz smiled, thinking their future looked promising.

Something clicked then in Liz's memory about David being seen on the third floor, and she playfully shook a finger at him. "So you really were only looking out my top floor windows for the view?"

David grinned. "Yes, and the best scenery was when I spotted these ladies coming across the square."

They said their goodbyes, and Liz stepped back from the buggy. Ruth turned and offered David the reins. He hesitated for a moment, then smiled and exchanged places with his mother. Sitting next to Ruth, David took the reins and they headed down the street.

Coming inside, Liz stepped over a sleeping Beans, grateful beyond measure for the good that had come out of the near tragic weekend. While her own mystery weekend had been a bust on many levels, seeing David reunited with his family—and a budding romance rekindled—colored her weekend in a much rosier hue.

She squatted beside Beans and ran a hand down his broad back. He opened his eyes without lifting his head, wagged his tail twice, gazed up at her with what appeared to be a wide smile, and then closed his eyes again with a contented sigh.

She passed on into the kitchen, wanting to relax with a magazine and a cup of coffee, but she could never unwind with Drew Garrett still in the building. She might as well do some spot cleaning while she waited for him to depart.

Wetting some paper towels, she attacked the brown spots and stains where people had dribbled coffee, plus the never-ending footprints people tracked in with their wet shoes. On her knees, she moved along the lower cupboards until she came to the built-in desk. Underneath it, pushed back against the wall, was an envelope. She pulled the desk chair away and reached back in the cubbyhole.

It was a bank envelope, wrinkled and creased, but intact. She peered inside. Sarah's missing wages! After a quick count, it appeared that all the money was there.

Liz sat cross-legged on the cold, hard floor, puzzled. How had it ended up there? But then she studied the envelope more closely. Those little creases and dents were chew marks. Beans's teeth marks, to be precise. How had Beans ended up with the wages envelope?

And then she remembered. On Friday morning, Sadie had knocked a stack of papers off the kitchen desk. The wages envelope must have landed so far back she hadn't seen it when she picked up everything else. She might have missed it, but it had been on Beans's eye level. Apparently he'd chewed on it, found it less tasty than his kibble, and left it where he'd found it.

At least she had the money back. That was the second positive thing to happen that day.

But then, as if to burst her bubble, she heard plodding steps on the staircase. Though tempted to hurry into her private quarters before Drew spotted her from the rotunda, she got to her feet and stood her ground. She'd much rather let him check himself out and just leave, but she wouldn't run from him. She reminded herself firmly that she had done nothing wrong and had no reason to avoid him.

"Ah, you're back." He stood in the kitchen doorway. "I was waiting for you."

Liz faced the dishonest man who'd written a rotten review of her inn.

She took a deep breath to tell him so, but then she remembered. She had already witnessed too much this weekend of Penny and Louise holding festering grudges and the pain they had caused everyone involved, including giving themselves a bleak future. Then a few minutes ago she'd observed something quite different in that Amish buggy parked out front. She'd witnessed through David's situation how forgiving old hurts could lead to healing and hope for what lay ahead.

The choice was hers, Liz realized. She could go either way with this deceitful reviewer. She breathed deeply, then made a conscious decision to let go of her resentment. In fact, she'd go one step further.

"Could I cook you some quick, authentic Amish food before you hit the road?"

He hesitated, disbelief evident on his face.

"Brown sugar oatmeal pancakes? Dutch squash biscuits?" she asked. "It's what I'd planned to fix for you tomorrow."

"I need to leave now, but thank you for offering." He cleared his throat as he set his suitcase on the floor at his feet. "I wanted to tell you that I thought about what you said. I've decided not to publish the review I wrote this weekend."

"Really?" Liz took a quick breath, at a total loss for words. "Thank you," she finally said. "I appreciate it."

He waved away her thanks. "If I can, I'll return for a couple days before my B&B book manuscript is due and I'll soak up that Amish experience."

"Thank you." Liz watched the reviewer leave and smiled in genuine contentment.

Like David, she was grateful for a second chance.

Up to this point, we've been doing all the writing. Now it's *your* turn!

Tell us what you think about this book, the characters, the bad guy, or anything else you'd like to share with us about this series. We can't wait to hear from *you*!

Log on to give us your feedback at:
https://www.surveymonkey.com/r/AmishInn

Annie's FICTION

Learn more about Annie's fiction books at

AnniesFiction.com

We've designed the Annie's Fiction
website especially for you!

Access your e-books and audiobooks • Manage your account

Choose from one of these great series:

Amish Inn Mysteries

Annie's Attic Mysteries

Annie's Mysteries Unraveled

Annie's Quilted Mysteries

Annie's Secrets of the Quilt

Annie's Sweet Intrigue

Antique Shop Mysteries

Chocolate Shoppe Mysteries

Creative Woman Mysteries

Hearts of Amish Country

Inn at Magnolia Harbor

Secrets of the Castleton Manor Library

Scottish Bakehouse Mysteries

Victorian Mansion Flower Shop Mysteries

What are you waiting for? Visit us
now at **AnniesFiction.com!**